Let the game begin!

Barney Northrup was a good salesman. In one day he had rented all of Sunset Towers to the people whose names were already printed on the mailboxes in an alcove off the lobby:

OFFICE	❑	*Dr. Wexler*
LOBBY	❑	*Theodorakis Coffee Shop*
2C	❑	*F. Baumbach*
2D	❑	*Theodorakis*
3C	❑	*S. Pulaski*
3D	❑	*Wexler*
4C	❑	*Hoo*
4D	❑	*J. J. Ford*
5	❑	*Shin Hoo's Restaurant*

Who were these people, these specially selected tenants? They were mothers and fathers and children. A dressmaker, a secretary, an inventor, a doctor, a judge. One was a bookie, one was a burglar, one was a bomber, and one was a mistake. Barney Northrup had rented one of the apartments to the wrong person.

Sunset Towers was a quiet, well-run building. Neighbor greeted neighbor with "Good morning" or a friendly smile, and grappled with small problems behind closed doors. The big problems were yet to come.

■ ■ ■ ■ ■ ■ ■ ■ ■ ■ ■

★"Raskin is an arch storyteller here. . . . Amazingly imaginative, with a cutting edge." . —*Booklist*, starred review

"A fascinating medley of word games, disguises, multiple aliases, and subterfuges—a demanding but rewarding book."
—*The Horn Book*

"Great fun for those who enjoy illusion, word play, or sleight of hand." —*The New York Times Book Review*

THE WESTING GAME

ELLEN RASKIN

PUFFIN BOOKS

PUFFIN BOOKS
An imprint of Penguin Random House LLC, New York

First published in the United States of America by E.P. Dutton,
a division of Penguin Books USA, Inc., 1978
First paperback edition published by Puffin Books 1992
Reissued 1997
Puffin Modern Classics edition published 2004
This paperback edition published 2021

Puffin Books & colophon are registered trademarks of Penguin Books Limited.

Visit us online at penguinrandomhouse.com.

THE LIBRARY OF CONGRESS HAS CATALOGED THE PREVIOUS PUFFIN BOOKS EDITION AS FOLLOWS:
Names: Raskin, Ellen, author.
Title: The Westing game / Ellen Raskin
Description: New York : Puffin Books, 2020. | Audience: Ages 8-12. | Audience: Grades 4-6. |
Summary: The mysterious death of an eccentric millionaire brings together an unlikely assortment
of heirs who must uncover the circumstances of his death before they can claim their inheritance.
Identifiers: LCCN 2020006673 | ISBN 9780593118108 (paperback) | ISBN 9780593204504 (ebook)
Subjects: CYAC: Inheritance and succession—Fiction. | Apartment houses—Fiction. |
Chicago (Ill.)—Fiction. | Mystery and detective stories. | Humorous stories.
Classification: LCC PZ7.R1817 We 2020 | DDC [Fic]—dc23
LC record available at https://lccn.loc.gov/2020006673

This edition ISBN 9780593526712

Printed in the United States of America

1 2 3 4 5 6 7 8 9 10

COMR

Text set in Apollo MT

■ **FOR JENNY**
who asked for a puzzle-mystery
■ **AND SUSAN K.**

THE WESTING GAME

1

THE SUN SETS in the west (just about everyone knows that), but Sunset Towers faced east. Strange!

Sunset Towers faced east and had no towers. This glittery, glassy apartment house stood alone on the Lake Michigan shore five stories high. Five empty stories high.

Then one day (it happened to be the Fourth of July), a most uncommon-looking delivery boy rode around town slipping letters under the doors of the chosen tenants-to-be. The letters were signed *Barney Northrup*.

The delivery boy was sixty-two years old, and there was no such person as Barney Northrup.

■ ■ ■ ■ ■ ■ ■ ■ ■ ■-■

Dear Lucky One:

Here it is—the apartment you've always dreamed of, at a
rent you can afford, in the newest, most luxurious building
on Lake Michigan:

SUNSET TOWERS

- Picture windows in every room
- Uniformed doorman, maid service
- Central air conditioning, hi-speed elevator
- Exclusive neighborhood, near excellent schools
- Etc., etc.

You have to see it to believe it. But these unbelievably elegant apartments will be shown by appointment only. So
hurry, there are only a few left!!! Call me now at 276-7474
for this once-in-a-lifetime offer.

Your servant,
Barney Northrup

P.S. I am also renting ideal space for:

- Doctor's office in lobby
- Coffee shop with entrance from parking lot
- Hi-class restaurant on entire top floor

■ ■ ■ ■ ■ ■ ■ ■ ■ ■ ■

Six letters were delivered, just six. Six appointments were made,
and one by one, family by family, talk, talk, talk, Barney Northrup led the tours around and about Sunset Towers.

"Take a look at all that glass. One-way glass," Barney Northrup said. "You can see out, nobody can see in."

Looking up, the Wexlers (the first appointment of the day)

were blinded by the blast of morning sun that flashed off the face of the building.

"See those chandeliers? Crystal!" Barney Northrup said, slicking his black moustache and straightening his hand-painted tie in the lobby's mirrored wall. "How about this carpeting? Three inches thick!"

"Gorgeous," Mrs. Wexler replied, clutching her husband's arm as her high heels wobbled in the deep plush pile. She, too, managed an approving glance in the mirror before the elevator door opened.

"You're really in luck," Barney Northrup said. "There's only one apartment left, but you'll love it. It was meant for you." He flung open the door to 3D. "Now, is that breathtaking, or is that breathtaking?"

Mrs. Wexler gasped; it was breathtaking, all right. Two walls of the living room were floor-to-ceiling glass. Following Barney Northrup's lead, she ooh-ed and aah-ed her joyous way through the entire apartment.

Her trailing husband was less enthusiastic. "What's this, a bedroom or a closet?" Jake Wexler asked, peering into the last room.

"It's a bedroom, of course," his wife replied.

"It looks like a closet."

"Oh Jake, this apartment is perfect for us, just perfect," Grace Wexler argued in a whining coo. The third bedroom was a trifle small, but it would do just fine for Turtle. "And think what it means having your office in the lobby, Jake; no more driving to and from work, no more mowing the lawn or shoveling snow."

"Let me remind you," Barney Northrup said, "the rent here is cheaper than what your old house costs in upkeep."

How would he know that, Jake wondered.

Grace stood before the front window where, beyond the road, beyond the trees, Lake Michigan lay calm and glistening. A lake view! Just wait until those so-called friends of hers with their classy houses see this place. The furniture would have to be reupholstered; no, she'd buy new furniture—beige velvet. And she'd have stationery made—blue with a deckle edge, her name and fancy address in swirling type across the top: *Grace Windsor Wexler, Sunset Towers on the Lake Shore.*

■ ■ ■ ■ ■ ■ ■ ■ ■ ■ ■ ■

Not every tenant-to-be was quite as overjoyed as Grace Windsor Wexler. Arriving in the late afternoon, Sydelle Pulaski looked up and saw only the dim, warped reflections of treetops and drifting clouds in the glass face of Sunset Towers.

"You're really in luck," Barney Northrup said for the sixth and last time. "There's only one apartment left, but you'll love it. It was meant for you." He flung open the door to a one-bedroom apartment in the rear. "Now, is that breathtaking or is that breathtaking?"

"Not especially," Sydelle Pulaski replied as she blinked into the rays of the summer sun setting behind the parking lot. She had waited all these years for a place of her own, and here it was, in an elegant building where rich people lived. But she wanted a lake view.

"The front apartments are taken," Barney Northrup said. "Besides, the rent's too steep for a secretary's salary. Believe me, you get the same luxuries here at a third of the price."

At least the view from the side window was pleasant. "Are you sure nobody can see in?" Sydelle Pulaski asked.

"Absolutely," Barney Northrup said, following her suspicious stare to the mansion on the north cliff. "That's just the old Westing house up there; it hasn't been lived in for fifteen years."

"Well, I'll have to think it over."

"I have twenty people begging for this apartment," Barney Northrup said, lying through his buckteeth. "Take it or leave it."

"I'll take it."

Whoever, whatever else he was, Barney Northrup was a good salesman. In one day he had rented all of Sunset Towers to the people whose names were already printed on the mailboxes in an alcove off the lobby:

OFFICE	❏	*Dr. Wexler*
LOBBY	❏	*Theodorakis Coffee Shop*
2C	❏	*F. Baumbach*
2D	❏	*Theodorakis*
3C	❏	*S. Pulaski*
3D	❏	*Wexler*
4C	❏	*Hoo*
4D	❏	*J. J. Ford*
5	❏	*Shin Hoo's Restaurant*

Who were these people, these specially selected tenants? They were mothers and fathers and children. A dressmaker, a secretary, an inventor, a doctor, a judge. And, oh yes, one was a bookie, one was a burglar, one was a bomber, and one was a mistake. Barney Northrup had rented one of the apartments to the wrong person.

■ GHOSTS OR WORSE ■

2 ON SEPTEMBER FIRST, the chosen ones (and the mistake) moved in. A wire fence had been erected along the north side of the building; on it a sign warned:

NO TRESPASSING—*Property of the Westing estate.*

The newly paved driveway curved sharply and doubled back on itself rather than breach the city-county line. Sunset Towers stood at the far edge of town.

On September second, Shin Hoo's Restaurant, specializing in authentic Chinese cuisine, held its grand opening. Only three people came. It was, indeed, an exclusive neighborhood; too exclusive for Mr. Hoo. However, the less expensive coffee shop that opened on the parking lot was kept busy serving breakfast, lunch, and dinner to tenants "ordering up" and to workers from nearby Westingtown.

Sunset Towers was a quiet, well-run building, and (except for the grumbling Mr. Hoo) the people who lived there seemed content. Neighbor greeted neighbor with "Good morning" or "Good evening" or a friendly smile, and grappled with small problems behind closed doors.

The big problems were yet to come.

■ ■ ■ ■ ■ ■ ■ ■ ■ ■ ■

Now it was the end of October. A cold, raw wind whipped dead leaves about the ankles of the four people grouped in the Sunset Towers driveway, but not one of them shivered. Not yet.

The stocky, broad-shouldered man in the doorman's uniform, standing with feet spread, fists on hips, was Sandy McSouthers. The two slim, trim high-school seniors, shielding their eyes against the stinging chill, were Theo Theodorakis and Doug Hoo. The small, wiry man pointing to the house on the hill was Otis Amber, the sixty-two-year-old delivery boy.

They faced north, gaping like statues cast in the moment of discovery, until Turtle Wexler, her kite tail of a braid flying behind her, raced her bicycle into the driveway. "Look! Look, there's smoke—there's smoke coming from the chimney of the Westing house."

The others had seen it. What did she think they were looking at anyway?

Turtle leaned on the handlebars, panting for breath. (Sunset Towers was near excellent schools, as Barney Northrup had promised, but the junior high was four miles away.) "Do you think—do you think old man Westing's up there?"

"Naw," Otis Amber, the old delivery boy, answered. "Nobody's seen him for years. Supposed to be living on a private island in the South Seas, he is; but most folks say he's dead.

6

Long-gone dead. They say his corpse is still up there in that big old house. They say his body is sprawled out on a fancy Oriental rug, and his flesh is rotting off those mean bones, and maggots are creeping in his eye sockets and crawling out his nose holes." The delivery boy added a high-pitched he-he-he to the gruesome details.

Now someone shivered. It was Turtle.

"Serves him right," Sandy said. At other times a cheery fellow, the doorman often complained bitterly about having been fired from his job of twenty years in the Westing paper mill. "But somebody must be up there. Somebody alive, that is." He pushed back the gold-braided cap and squinted at the house through his steel-framed glasses as if expecting the curling smoke to write the answer in the autumn air. "Maybe it's those kids again. No, it couldn't be."

"What kids?" the three kids wanted to know.

"Why, those two unfortunate fellas from Westingtown."

"What unfortunate fellas?" The three heads twisted from the doorman to the delivery boy. Doug Hoo ducked Turtle's whizzing braid. Touch her precious pigtail, even by accident, and she'll kick you in the shins, the brat. He couldn't chance an injury to his legs, not with the big meet coming. The track star began to jog in place.

"Horrible, it was horrible," Otis Amber said with a shudder that sent the loose straps of his leather aviator's helmet swinging about his long, thin face. "Come to think of it, it happened exactly one year ago tonight. On Halloween."

"What happened?" Theo Theodorakis asked impatiently. He was late for work in the coffee shop.

"Tell them, Otis," Sandy urged.

The delivery boy stroked the gray stubble on his pointed chin. "Seems it all started with a bet; somebody bet them a dollar they couldn't stay in that spooky house five minutes. One measly buck! The poor kids hardly got through those French doors on this side of the Westing house when they came tearing

7

out like they was being chased by a ghost. Chased by a ghost—or worse."

Or worse? Turtle forgot her throbbing toothache. Theo Theodorakis and Doug Hoo, older and more worldly-wise, exchanged winks but stayed to hear the rest of the story.

"One fella ran out crazy-like, screaming his head off. He never stopped screaming 'til he hit the rocks at the bottom of the cliff. The other fella hasn't said but two words since. Something about purple."

Sandy helped him out. "Purple waves."

Otis Amber nodded sadly. "Yep, that poor fella just sits in the state asylum saying, 'Purple waves, purple waves' over and over again, and his scared eyes keep staring at his hands. You see, when he came running out of the Westing house, his hands was dripping with warm, red blood."

Now all three shivered.

"Poor kid," the doorman said. "All that pain and suffering for a dollar bet."

"Make it two dollars for each minute I stay in there, and you're on," Turtle said.

■ ■ ■ ■ ■ ■ ■ ■ ■ ■ ■ ■

Someone was spying on the group in the driveway.

From the front window of apartment 2D, fifteen-year-old Chris Theodorakis watched his brother Theo shake hands (it must be a bet) with the skinny, one-pigtailed girl and rush into the lobby. The family coffee shop would be busy now; his brother should have been working the counter half an hour ago. Chris checked the wall clock. Two more hours before Theo would bring up his dinner. Then he would tell him about the limper.

Earlier that afternoon Chris had followed the flight of a purple martin (*Progne subis*) across the field of brambles, through the oaks, up to the red maple on the hill. The bird flew off, but something else caught his eye. Someone (he could not tell if the person was a man or a woman) came out of the shadows on the lawn, unlocked the French doors, and disappeared into the Westing house. Someone with a limp. Minutes later smoke began to rise from the chimney.

Once again Chris turned toward the side window and scanned the house on the cliff. The French doors were closed; heavy drapes hung full against the seventeen windows he had counted so many times.

They didn't need drapes on the special glass windows here in Sunset Towers. He could see out, but nobody could see in. Then why did he sometimes feel that someone was watching him? Who could be watching him? God? If God was watching, then why was he like this?

The binoculars fell to the boy's lap. His head jerked, his body coiled, lashed by violent spasms. Relax, Theo will come soon. Relax, soon the geese will be flying south in a V. Canada goose (*Branta canadensis*). Relax. Relax and watch the wind tangle the smoke and blow it toward Westingtown.

■ TENANTS IN AND OUT ■

3 UPSTAIRS IN 3D Angela Wexler stood on a hassock as still and blank-faced pretty as a store-window dummy. Her pale blue eyes stared unblinkingly at the lake.

"Turn, dear," said Flora Baumbach, the dressmaker, who lived and worked in a smaller apartment on the second floor.

Angela pivoted in a slow quarter turn. "Oh!"

Startled by the small cry, Flora Baumbach dropped the pin from her pudgy fingers and almost swallowed the three in her mouth.

"Please be careful, Mrs. Baumbach; my Angela has very delicate skin." Grace Windsor Wexler was supervising the fitting of her daughter's wedding dress from the beige velvet couch. Above her hung the two dozen framed flower prints she had

9

selected and arranged with the greatest of taste and care. She could have been an interior decorator, a good one, too, if it wasn't for the pressing demands of so on and so forth.

"Mrs. Baumbach didn't prick me, Mother," Angela said evenly. "I was just surprised to see smoke coming from the Westing house chimney."

Crawling with slow caution on her hands and knees, Flora Baumbach paused in the search for the dropped pin to peer up through her straight gray bangs.

Mrs. Wexler set her coffee cup on the driftwood coffee table and craned her neck for a better view. "We must have new neighbors; I'll have to drive up there with a housewarming gift; they may need some decorating advice."

"Hey, look! There's smoke coming from the Westing house!" Again Turtle was late with the news.

"Oh, it's you." Mrs. Wexler always seemed surprised to see her other daughter, so unlike golden-haired, angel-faced Angela.

Flora Baumbach, about to rise with the found pin, quickly sank down again to protect her sore shin in the shag carpeting. She had pulled Turtle's braid in the lobby yesterday.

"Otis Amber says that old man Westing's stinking corpse is rotting on an Oriental rug."

"My, oh my," Flora Baumbach exclaimed, and Mrs. Wexler clicked her tongue in an irritated "tsk."

Turtle decided not to go on with the horror story. Not that her mother cared if she got killed or ended up a raving lunatic. "Mrs. Baumbach, could you hem my witch's costume? I need it for tonight."

Mrs. Wexler answered. "Can't you see she's busy with Angela's wedding dress? And why must you wear a silly costume like that? Really, Turtle, I don't know why you insist on making yourself ugly."

"It's no sillier than a wedding dress," Turtle snapped back. "Besides, nobody gets married anymore, and if they do, they don't wear silly wedding dresses." She was close to a tantrum. "Besides, who would want to marry that stuck-up-know-it-all-marshmallow-face-doctor-denton . . . ?"

"That's enough of your smart mouth!" Mrs. Wexler leaped up, hand ready to strike; instead she straightened a framed flower print, patted her fashionable honey-blonde hairdo, and sat down again. She had never hit Turtle, but one of these days—besides, a stranger was present. "Doctor Deere is a brilliant young man," she explained for Flora Baumbach's ears. The dressmaker smiled politely. "Angela will soon be Angela Deere; isn't that a precious name?" The dressmaker nodded. "And then we'll have two doctors in the family. Now where do you think you're going?"

Turtle was at the front door. "Downstairs to tell daddy about the smoke coming from the Westing house."

"Come back this instant. You know your father operates in the afternoon; why don't you go to your room and work on stock market reports or whatever you do in there."

"Some room, it's even too small for a closet."

"I'll hem your witch's costume, Turtle," Angela offered.

Mrs. Wexler beamed on her perfect child draped in white. "What an angel."

■ ■ ■ ■ ■ ■ ■ ■ ■ ■ ■ ■

Crow's clothes were black; her skin, dead white. She looked severe. Rigid, in fact. Rigid and righteously severe. No one could have guessed that under that stern facade her stomach was doing flip-flops as Doctor Wexler cut out a corn.

Staring down at the fine lines of pink scalp that showed through the podiatrist's thinning light brown hair did nothing to ease her queasiness; so, softly humming a hymn, she settled her gaze on the north window. "Smoke!"

"Watch it!" Jake Wexler almost cut off her little toe along with the corn.

Unaware of the near amputation, the cleaning woman stared at the Westing house.

"If you will just sit back," Jake began, but his patient did not hear him. She must have been a handsome woman at one time, but life had used her harshly. Her faded hair, knotted in a tight bun on the nape of her gaunt neck, glinted gold-red in the light. Her profile was fine, marred only by the jut of her clenched jaw. Well, let's get on with it, Friday was his busy day, he had phone calls to make. "Please sit back, Mrs. Crow. I'm almost finished."

"What?"

Jake gently replaced her foot on the chair's pedestal. "I see you've hurt your shin."

"What?" For an instant their eyes met; then she looked away. A shy creature (or a guilty one), Crow averted her face when she spoke. "Your daughter Turtle kicked me," she muttered, staring once again at the Westing house. "That's what happens when there is no religion in the home. Sandy says Westing's corpse is up there, rotting away on an Oriental rug, but I don't believe it. If he's truly dead, then he's roasting in hell. We are sinners, all."

■ ■ ■ ■ ■ ■ ■ ■ ■ ■ ■ ■

"What do you mean his corpse is rotting on an Oriental rug, some kind of Persian rug, maybe a Chinese rug." Mr. Hoo joined his son at the glass sidewall of the fifth-floor restaurant. "And why were you wasting precious time listening to an overaged delivery boy with an overactive imagination when you should have been studying." It was not a question; Doug's father never asked questions. "Don't shrug at me, go study."

"Sure, Dad." Doug jogged off through the kitchen; it was no use arguing that there was no school tomorrow, just track practice. He jogged down the back stairs; no matter what excuse he gave, "Go study," his father would say, "go study." He jogged into the Hoos' rear apartment, stretched out on the bare floor and repeated "Go study" to twenty sit-ups.

Only two customers were expected for the dinner hour (Shin Hoo's Restaurant could seat one hundred). Mr. Hoo slammed the reservations book shut, pressed a hand against the pain in his ample stomach, unwrapped a chocolate bar, and devoured it quickly before acid etched another ulcer. Back home again, is he. Well, Westing won't get off so easy this time, not on his life.

A small, delicate woman in a long white apron stood in silence before the restaurant's east window. She stared longingly into the boundless gray distance as if far, far on the other side of Lake Michigan lay China.

■ ■ ■ ■ ■ ■ ■ ■ ■ ■ ■

Sandy McSouthers saluted as the maroon Mercedes swung around the curved driveway and came to a stop at the entrance. He opened the car door with a ceremony reserved only for Judge J. J. Ford. "Look up there, Judge. There's smoke coming from the Westing house."

A tall black woman in a tailored suit, her short-clipped hair touched with gray, slipped out from behind the wheel, handed the car keys to the doorman, and cast a disinterested glance at the house on the hill.

"They say nobody's up there, just the corpse of old man Westing rotting away on an Oriental rug," Sandy reported as he hoisted a full briefcase from the trunk of the car. "Do you believe in ghosts, Judge?"

"There is certain to be a more rational explanation."

"You're right, of course, Judge." Sandy opened the heavy glass door and followed on the judge's heels through the lobby. "I was just repeating what Otis Amber said."

"Otis Amber is a stupid man, if not downright mad." J. J. Ford hurried into the elevator. She should not have said that, not her, not the first black, the first woman, to have been elected to a judgeship in the state. She was tired after a trying day, that was it. Or was it? So Sam Westing has come home at last. Well, she could sell the car, take out a bank loan, pay him back—in cash. But would he take it? "Please don't repeat what I said about Otis Amber, Mr. McSouthers."

"Don't worry, Judge." The doorman escorted her to the door of apartment 4D. "What you tell me is strictly confidential." And it was. J. J. Ford was the biggest tipper in Sunset Towers.

■ ■ ■ ■ ■ ■ ■ ■ ■ ■ ■

"I saw someb-b-b . . ." Chris Theodorakis was too excited to stutter out the news to his brother. One arm shot out and twisted up over his head. Dumb arm.

Theo squatted next to the wheelchair. "Listen, Chris, I'll tell you about that haunted castle on the hill." His voice was soothing and hushed in mystery. "Somebody is up there, Chris, but nobody is there, just rich Mr. Westing, and he's dead. Dead as a squashed June bug and rotting away on a moth-eaten Oriental rug."

Chris relaxed as he always did when his brother told him a story. Theo was good at making up stories.

"And the worms are crawling in and out of the dead man's skull, in and out of his ear holes, his nose holes, his mouth holes, in and out of all his holes."

Chris laughed, then quickly composed his face. He was supposed to look scared.

Theo leaned closer. "And high above the putrid corpse a crystal chandelier is tinkling. It tinkles and twinkles, but not one breath of air stirs in that gloomy tomb of a room."

Gloomy tomb of a room—Theo will make a good writer someday, Chris thought. He wouldn't spoil this wonderful, spooky Halloween story by telling him about the real person up there, the one with the limp.

So Chris sat quietly, his body at ease, and heard about ghosts and ghouls and purple waves, and smiled at his brother with pure delight.

"A smile that could break your heart," Sydelle Pulaski, the

tenant in 3c, always said. But no one paid any attention to Sydelle Pulaski.

■ ■ ■ ■ ■ ■ ■ ■ ■ ■ ■ ■

Sydelle Pulaski struggled out of the taxi, large end first. She was not a heavy woman, just wide-hipped from years of secretarial sitting. If only there was a ladylike way to get out of a cab. Her green rhinestone-studded glasses slipped down her fleshy nose as she grappled with a tall triangular package and a stuffed shopping bag. If only that lazy driver would lend her a hand.

Not for a nickel tip, he wouldn't. The cabbie slammed the back door and sped around the curved driveway, narrowly missing the Mercedes that Sandy was driving to the parking lot.

At least the never-there-when-you-need-him doorman had propped open the front door. Not that he ever helped her, or noticed her, for that matter.

No one ever noticed. Sydelle Pulaski limped through the lobby. She could be carrying a high-powered rifle in that package and no one would notice. She had moved to Sunset Towers hoping to meet elegant people, but no one had invited her in for so much as a cup of tea. No one paid any attention to her, except that poor crippled boy whose smile could break your heart, and that bratty kid with the braid—she'll be sorry she kicked her in the shin.

Juggling her load, earrings jingling and charm bracelet jangling, Sydelle Pulaski unlocked the several locks to apartment 3c and bolted the door behind her. There'd be fewer burglaries around here if people listened to her about putting in dead-bolt locks. But nobody listened. Nobody cared.

On the plastic-covered dining table she set out the contents of the shopping bag: six cans of enamel, paint thinner, and brushes. She unwrapped the long package and leaned four wooden crutches against the wall. The sun was setting over the parking lot, but Sydelle Pulaski did not look out her back window. From the side window smoke could be seen rising from the Westing house, but Sydelle Pulaski did not notice.

"No one ever notices Sydelle Pulaski," she muttered, "but now they will. Now they will."

4 THE HALLOWEEN MOON was full. Except for her receding chin Turtle Wexler looked every inch the witch, her dark unbraided hair streaming wild in the wind from under her peaked hat, a putty wart pasted on her small beaked nose. If only she could fly to the Westing house on a broomstick instead of scrambling over rocks on all fours, what with all she had to carry. Under the long black cape the pockets of her jeans bulged with necessities for the night's dangerous vigil.

Doug Hoo had already reached the top of the cliff and taken his station behind the maple on the lawn. (The track star was chosen timekeeper because he could run faster than anyone in the state of Wisconsin.) Here she comes, it's about time. Shivering knee-deep in damp leaves that couldn't do his leg muscles much good, he readied his thumb on the button of the stopwatch.

Turtle squinted into the blackness that lay within the open French doors. Open, as though someone or some *Thing* was expecting her. There's no such thing as a ghost; besides, all you had to do was speak friendly-like to them. (Ghosts, like dogs, know when a person's scared.) Ghosts or worse, Otis Amber had said. Well, not even the "worse" could hurt Turtle Wexler. She was pure of heart and deed; she only kicked shins in self-defense, so that couldn't count against her. She wasn't scared; she was not scared.

"Hurry up!" That was Doug from behind the tree.

At two dollars a minute, twenty-five minutes would pay for a subscription to *The Wall Street Journal*. She could stay all night.

She was prepared. Turtle checked her pockets: two sandwiches, Sandy's flask filled with orange pop, a flashlight, her mother's silver cross to ward off vampires. The putty wart on her nose (soaked in Angela's perfume in the event she was locked up with the stinking corpse) was clogging her nostrils with sticky sweetness. Turtle took a deep breath of chill night air and flinched with pain. She was afraid of dentists, not ghosts or . . . don't think about purple waves, think about two dollars a minute. Now, one—two—three—three and a half—GO!

Doug checked his stopwatch. Nine minutes.

Ten minutes.

Eleven minutes.

Suddenly a terrified scream—a young girl's scream—pierced the night. Should he go in, or was this one of the brat's tricks? Another scream, closer.

"E-E-E-e-e-e-e-e-e-e!" Clutching the bunched cape around her waist, Turtle came hurtling out of the Westing house. "E-e-e-e-e-e-e-e-e!"

■ ■ ■ ■ ■ ■ ■ ■ ■ ■ ■

Turtle had seen the corpse in the Westing house, but it was not rotting and it was not sprawled on an Oriental rug. The dead man was tucked in a four-poster bed.

A throbbing whisper, "Pur-ple, pur-ple" (or was it "Tur-tle, Tur-tle"—whatever it was, it was scary), had beckoned her to the master bedroom on the second floor, and . . .

Maybe it was a dream. No, it couldn't be; she ached all over from the tumble down the stairs.

The moon was down, the window dark. Turtle lay in the narrow bed in her narrow room, waiting (dark, still dark), waiting. At last slow morning crept up the cliff and raised the Westing house, the house of whispers, the house of death. Two dollars times twelve minutes equals twenty-four dollars.

Thud! The morning newspaper was flung against the front

door. Turtle tiptoed through the sleeping apartment to retrieve it and climbed back into bed, the dead man staring at her from the front page. The face was younger; the short beard, darker; but it was he, all right.

SAM WESTING FOUND DEAD

Found? No one else knew about the bedded-down corpse except Doug, and he had not believed her. Then who found the body? The whisperer?

> Samuel W. Westing, the mysterious industrialist who disappeared thirteen years ago, was found dead in his Westingtown mansion last night. He was sixty-five years old.
>
> The only child of immigrant parents, orphaned at the age of twelve, self-educated, hard-working Samuel Westing saved his laborer's wages and bought a small paper mill. From these meager beginnings he built the giant Westing Paper Products Corporation and founded the city of Westingtown to house his thousands of workers and their families. His estate is estimated to be worth over two hundred million dollars.

Turtle read that again: two hundred million dollars. Wow!

> When asked the secret of his success, the industrialist always replied: "Clean living, hard work, and fair play." Westing set his own example; he neither drank nor smoked and never gambled. Yet he was a dedicated gamesman and a master at chess.

Turtle had been in the game room. That's where she picked up the billiard cue she had carried up the stairs as a weapon.

A great patriot, Samuel Westing was famous for his fun-filled Fourth of July celebrations. Whether disguised as Ben Franklin or a lowly drummer boy, he always acted a role in the elaborately staged pageants which he wrote and directed. Perhaps best remembered was his surprise portrayal of Betsy Ross.

Games and feasting followed the pageant, and at sunset Mr. Westing put on his Uncle Sam costume and set off fireworks from his front lawn. The spectacular pyrotechnic display could be viewed thirty miles away.

Fireworks! So that's what was in those boxes stamped *Danger—explosives* stacked in the ground-floor storeroom. What a "pyrotechnic display" that would make if they all went off at the same time.

The paper king's later years were marred by tragedy. His only daughter, Violet, drowned on the eve of her wedding, and two years later his troubled wife deserted their home. Although Mr. Westing obtained a divorce, he never remarried.

Five years later he was sued by an inventor over rights to the disposable paper diaper. On his way to court Samuel Westing and his friend, Dr. Sidney Sikes, were involved in a near-fatal automobile accident. Both men were hospitalized with severe injuries. Sikes resumed his Westingtown medical practice and the post of county coroner, but Westing disappeared from sight.

It was rumored, but never confirmed, that he controlled the vast Westing Paper Products Corporation from a private island in the South Seas. He is still listed as chairman of the board.

"We are as surprised as you are, and deeply sad-dened," a spokesman for Julian R. Eastman, President and Chief Executive Officer of the corporation, stated when informed that Westing's body was found in his lakeside home. Dr. Sikes' response was: "A tragic end to a tragic life. Sam Westing was a truly great and important man."

The funeral will be private. The executor of the Westing estate said the deceased requested that, in place of flowers, donations be sent to Blind Bowlers of America.

Turtle turned the page of the newspaper, but that was all. That was all?

There was no mention of how the body was found.

There was no mention of the envelope propped on the bedside table on which a shaky hand had scrawled: *If I am found dead in bed.* She had been edging her way against the four-poster, read-ing the words in the beam of the flashlight, when she felt the hand, the waxy dead hand that lay on the red, white, and blue quilt. Through her scream she had seen the white-bearded face. She remembered running, tripping over the billiard cue, falling down the stairs, denting Sandy's flask, and dropping everything else.

There was no mention of two suspicious peanut butter and jelly sandwiches on the premises, or a flashlight, or a silver cross on a chain.

There was no mention of prowlers; no mention of anyone hav-ing seen a witch; no mention of footprints on the lawn: track shoes and sneakers size six.

Oh well, she had nothing to fear (other than losing her moth-er's cross). Old Mr. Westing probably died of a heart attack—or pneumonia—it was drafty in there. Turtle hid the folded news-paper in her desk drawer, counted her black-and-blue marks in the mirror (seven), dressed, and set out to find the four people who knew she had been in the Westing house last night: Doug Hoo, Theo Theodorakis, Otis Amber, and Sandy. They owed her twenty-four dollars.

■ ■ ■ ■ ■ ■ ■ ■ ■ ■ ■ ■

At noon the sixty-two-year-old delivery boy began his rounds. He had sixteen letters to deliver from E. J. Plum, Attorney-at-Law. Otis Amber knew what the letters said, because one was addressed to him:

> As a named beneficiary in the estate
> of Samuel W. Westing, your attendance
> is required in the south library of the
> Westing house tomorrow at 4 p.m. for
> the reading of the will.

"Means old man Westing left you some money," he explained. "Just sign this receipt here. What do you mean, what does 'position' mean? It means position, like a job. Most receipts have that to make sure the right person gets the right letter."

Grace Windsor Wexler wrote *housewife,* crossed it out, wrote *decorator,* crossed it out, and wrote *heiress.* Then she wanted to know "Who else? How many? How much?"

"I ain't allowed to say nothing."

The other heirs were too stunned by the unexpected legacy to bother him with questions. Madame Hoo marked an *X* and her husband filled in her name and position. Theo wanted to sign the receipt for his brother, but Chris insisted on doing it himself. Slowly, taking great pains, he wrote *Christos Theodorakis, bird-watcher.*

By the time the sun had set behind the Sunset Towers parking lot, Otis Amber, *deliverer,* had completed his rounds.

5 THE MARBLED SKY lay heavy on the gray Great Lake when Grace Windsor Wexler parked her car in the Westing driveway and strode up the walk ahead of her daughters. Her husband had refused to come, but no matter. Recalling family gossip about a rich uncle (maybe it was a great-uncle—anyway, his name was Sam), Grace had convinced herself that she was the rightful heir. (Jake was Jewish, so he could not possibly be related to Samuel W. Westing.)

"I can't imagine what became of my silver cross," she said, fingering the gold-link necklace under her mink stole as she paused to appraise the big house. "You know, Angela, we could have the wedding right here. . . . Turtle, where are you wandering off to now?"

"The letter said— Never mind." Turtle preferred not to explain how she knew the library could be entered from the French doors on the lawn.

The front door was opened by Crow. Although the Sunset Towers cleaning woman always wore black, here it reminded Grace Wexler to dab at her eyes with a lace handkerchief. This was a house of mourning.

The silent Crow helped Angela with her coat and nodded approval of her blue velvet dress with white collar and cuffs.

"I'll keep my furs with me," Grace said. She did not want to be taken for one of the poor relatives. "Seems rather chilly in here."

Turtle, too, complained of the chill, but her mother tugged off her coat to reveal a fluffy, ruffly pink party dress two sizes too large and four inches too long. It was one of Angela's hand-me-downs.

"Please sit anywhere," the lawyer said without glancing from the envelopes he was sorting at the head of the long library table.

Mrs. Wexler took the chair to his right and motioned to her favorite. Angela sat down next to her mother, removed a trousseau towel from her large tapestry shoulder bag, and took up embroidering the monogram D. Slumped in the third chair, Turtle pretended she had never seen this paneled library with its bare and dusty shelves. Suddenly she sat up with a start. An open coffin draped in bunting rested on a raised platform at the far corner of the room; in it lay the dead man, looking exactly as she had found him, except now he was dressed in the costume of Uncle Sam—including the tall hat. Between the waxy hands, folded across his chest, lay her mother's silver cross.

Grace Wexler was too busy greeting the next heir to notice. "Why Doctor D., I had no idea you'd be here; but of course, you'll soon be a member of the family. Come, sit next to your bride-to-be; Turtle, you'll have to move down."

D. Denton Deere, always in a hurry, brushed a quick kiss on Angela's cheek. He was still wearing his hospital whites.

"I didn't know this was a pajama party," Turtle said, relinquishing her chair and stomping to the far end of the table.

■ ■ ■ ■ ■ ■ ■ ■ ■ ■ ■ ■

The next heir, short and round, entered timidly, her lips pressed together in an impish smile that curved up to what must be pointed ears under her straight-cut, steely hair.

"Hello, Mrs. Baumbach," Angela said. "I don't think you've met my fiancé, Denton Deere."

"You're a lucky man, Mr. Deere."

"*Doctor* Deere," Mrs. Wexler corrected her, puzzled by the dressmaker's presence.

"Yes, of course, I'm so sorry." Sensing that she was unwelcome at this end of the room, Flora Baumbach walked on. "Hi, mind if I sit next to you? I promise not to pull your braid."

"That's okay." Turtle was hunched over the table, her small chin resting between her crossed arms. From there she could see everything except the coffin.

Grace Wexler dismissed the next heir with an audible tongue click. That distasteful little man didn't even have the sense to remove his silly aviator's cap. "Tsk." And what in heaven's name was he doing here?

The delivery boy shouted: "Let's give a cheer, Otis Amber is here!" Turtle laughed, Flora Baumbach tittered, and Grace Wexler again clicked her tongue, "Tsk!"

Doug Hoo and his father entered silently, but Sandy gave a hearty "Hi!" and a cheery wave. He wore his doorman's uniform, but unlike Otis Amber, carried his hat in his hand.

Grace Windsor Wexler was no longer surprised at the odd assortment of heirs. Household workers, all, or former employees, she decided. The rich always reward servants in their wills, and her Uncle Sam was a generous man. "Aren't your parents coming?" she asked the older Theodorakis boy as he wheeled his brother into the library.

"They weren't invited," Theo replied.

"Itsss-oo-nn," Chris announced.

"What did he say?"

"He said it's snowing," Theo and Flora Baumbach explained at the same time.

The heirs watched helplessly as the invalid's thin frame was suddenly torn and twisted by convulsions. Only the dressmaker rushed to his side. "I know, I know," she simpered, "you were trying to tell us about the itsy-bitsy snowflings."

Theo moved her away. "My brother is not an infant, and he's not retarded, so please, no more baby talk."

Blinking away tears, Flora Baumbach returned to her seat, the elfin smile still painted on her pained face.

Some stared at the afflicted child with morbid fascination, but most turned away. They didn't want to see.

"Pyramidal tract involvement," Denton Deere whispered, trying to impress Angela with his diagnosis.

Angela, her face a mirror to the boy's suffering, grabbed her tapestry bag and hurried out of the room.

■ ■ ■ ■ ■ ■ ■ ■ ■ ■ ■ ■

"Why hello, Judge Ford." Proud of her liberalism, Grace Windsor Wexler stood and leaned over the table to shake the black woman's hand. She must be here in some legal capacity, or maybe her mother was a household maid, but of one thing Grace was certain: J. J. Ford could no more be related to Samuel W. Westing than Mr. Hoo.

"Can't we get started?" Mr. Hoo asked, hoping to get back in time to watch the football game on television. "I must return to my restaurant," he announced loudly. "Sunday is our busy day, but we are still accepting reservations. Shin Hoo's Restaurant on the fifth floor of Sunset Towers, specializing in . . ."

Doug tugged at his father's sleeve. "Not here, Dad; not in front of the dead."

"What dead?" Mr. Hoo had not noticed the open coffin. Now he did. "Ohhh!"

The lawyer explained that several heirs had not yet arrived. "My wife is not coming," said Mr. Hoo. Grace said, "Doctor Wexler was called away on an emergency operation."

"An emergency Packers game in Green Bay," Turtle confided to Flora Baumbach, who scrunched up her shoulders and tittered behind a plump hand.

"Then we are still waiting for one, no, two more," the lawyer said, fumbling with his papers, his hands shaking under the strict scrutiny of the judge.

Judge Ford had recognized E. J. Plum. Several months ago he had argued before her court, bumbling to the point of incompetence. Why, she wondered, was a young, inexperienced attorney chosen to handle an estate of such importance? Come to think of it, what was *she* doing here? Curiosity? Perhaps, but what about the rest of them, the other tenants of Sunset Towers? Don't anticipate, Josie-Jo, wait for Sam Westing to make the first move.

Light footsteps were heard in the hall. It was only Angela, who blushed and, hugging her tapestry bag close to her body, returned to her seat.

The heirs waited. Some chatted with neighbors, some looked

up at the gilt ceiling, some studied the pattern of the Oriental rug. Judge Ford stared at the table, at Theo Theodorakis's hand. A calloused hand, a healed cut, the shiny slash of a burn on the deep bronze skin. She lowered her hands to her lap. His Greek skin was darker than her "black" skin.

■ ■ ■ ■ ■ ■ ■ ■ ■ ■ ■

Thump, thump, thump. Someone was coming, or were there two of them?

In came Crow. Eyes lowered, without a word, she sat down next to Otis Amber. A dark cloud passed from her face as she eased off a tight shoe under the table.

Thump, thump, thump. The last expected heir arrived.

"Hello, everybody. Sorry I'm late. I haven't quite adjusted to this"—Sydelle Pulaski waved a gaily painted crutch in the air, tottered, and set it down quickly with another thump—"this crutch. Crutch. What a horrible word, but I guess I'll have to get used to it." She pursed her bright red mouth, painted to a fullness beyond the narrow line of her lips, trying to suppress a smile of triumph. Everyone was staring; she knew they would notice.

"What happened, Pulaski?" Otis Amber asked. "Did you pull Turtle's braid again?"

"More likely she visited Wexler the foot butcher," Sandy suggested.

Sydelle was pleased to hear someone come to her defense with a loud click of the tongue. She had not even blinked a false eyelash at those offensive remarks (poise, they call it). "It's really nothing," she reported bravely, "just some sort of wasting disease. But pity me not, I shall live out my remaining time enjoying each precious day to the full." Thump, thump, thump. The secretary kept to the side of the room, avoiding the Oriental rug that might cushion the thump of her purple-striped crutch, as she made her way to the end of the table. Her exaggerated hips were even more exaggerated by the wavy stripes of white on her purple dress.

Purple waves, Turtle thought.

Denton Deere almost fell off his chair, leaning back to follow this most unusual case. First she favored her left leg, then her right leg.

"What is it?" whispered Mrs. Wexler.

The intern did not have the least notion, but he had to say something. "Traveling sporadic myositis," he pronounced quickly and glanced at Angela. Her eyes remained on her embroidery.

The lawyer stood, documents in hand, and cleared his throat several times. Grace Windsor Wexler, her chin tilted in the regal pose of an heiress, gave him her full attention.

"One minute, please." Sydelle Pulaski propped her purple-and-white-striped crutch against the table, then removed a shorthand pad and pencil from her handbag. "Thank you for waiting; you may begin."

■ THE WESTING WILL ■

6 "MY NAME," the young lawyer began, "is Edgar Jennings Plum. Although I never had the honor of meeting Samuel W. Westing, for some reason yet unexplained, I was appointed executor of this will found adjacent to the body of the deceased.

"Let me assure you that I have examined the documents at hand as thoroughly as possible in the short time available. I have verified the signatures to be those of Samuel W. Westing and his two witnesses: Julian R. Eastman, President and Chief Executive Officer of Westing Paper Products Corporation, and Sidney Sikes, M.D., Coroner of Westing County. Although the will you are about to hear may seem eccentric, I pledge my good name and reputation on its legality."

Breathless with suspense, the heirs stared popeyed at Edgar Jennings Plum, who now coughed into his fist, now cleared his throat, now rustled papers, and now, at last, began to read aloud from the Westing will.

I, *SAMUEL W. WESTING, resident of Westing County in the fair state of Wisconsin in the great and glorious United States of America, being of sound mind and memory, do hereby declare this to be my last will and testament.*

FIRST • *I returned to live among my friends and my enemies. I came home to seek my heir, aware that in doing so I faced death. And so I did.*

Today I have gathered together my nearest and dearest, my sixteen nieces and nephews

"What!"

(Sit down, Grace Windsor Wexler!)

The lawyer stammered an apology to the still-standing woman. "I was only reading; I mean, those are Mr. Westing's words."

"If it's any comfort to you, Mrs. Wexler," Judge Ford remarked with biting dignity, "I am just as appalled by our purported relationship."

"Oh, I didn't mean . . ."

"Hey, Angela," Turtle called the length of the table. "It's against the law to marry that doctor-to-be. He's your cousin."

D. Denton Deere, patting Angela's hand in his best bedside manner, pricked his finger on her embroidery needle.

"I can't tell who said what with this chatter," Sydelle Pulaski complained. "Would you read that again, Mr. Lawyer?"

> Today I have gathered together my nearest and dear-
> est, my sixteen nieces and nephews (Sit down, Grace
> Windsor Wexler!) to view the body of your Uncle Sam
> for the last time.
>
> Tomorrow its ashes will be scattered to the four winds.

SECOND • *I, Samuel W. Westing, hereby swear that
I did not die of natural causes. My life was taken from
me—by one of you!*

"O-o-o-uggg." Chris's arm flailed the air, his accusing finger
pointed here, no, there; it pointed everywhere. His exaggerated
motions acted out the confusion shared by all but one of the
heirs as they looked around at the stunned faces of their neighbors to confirm what they heard. Rereading her notes, Sydelle
Pulaski now uttered a small shriek. "Eek!"

"Murder? Does that mean Westing was murdered?" Sandy
asked the heir on his left.

Crow turned away in silence.

"Does that mean murder?" he asked the heir on his right.

"Murder? Of course it means murder. Sam Westing was murdered," Mr. Hoo replied. "Either that or he ate once too often in
that greasy-spoon coffee shop."

Theo resented Hoo's slur on the family business. "It was murder, all right. And the will says the murderer is one of us." He
glared at the restaurant owner.

"Have the police been notified of the charge?" Judge Ford
asked the lawyer.

Plum shrugged. "I presume they will perform an autopsy."

The judge shook her head in dismay. Autopsy? Westing was
already embalmed; tomorrow he would be cremated.

> *The police are helpless. The culprit is far too cunning
> to be apprehended for this dastardly deed.*

"Oh my!" Flora Baumbach clapped a hand to her mouth on hearing "dastardly." First murder, now a swear word.

> *I, alone, know the name. Now it is up to you. Cast out the sinner, let the guilty rise and confess.*

"Amen," said Crow.

> THIRD • *Who among you is worthy to be the Westing heir? Help me. My soul shall roam restlessly until that one is found.*
>
> *The estate is at the crossroads. The heir who wins the windfall will be the one who finds the . . .*

"Ashes!" the doorman shouted. Some tittered to relieve the unbearable tension, some cast him a reproachful glance, Grace Wexler clicked her tongue, and Sydelle Pulaski shhh-ed. "It was just a joke," Sandy tried to explain. "You know, ashes scattered to the winds, so the one who wins the windfall gets— Oh, never mind."

> FOURTH • *Hail to thee, O land of opportunity! You have made me, the son of poor immigrants, rich, powerful, and respected.*
>
> *So take stock in America, my heirs, and sing in praise of this generous land. You, too, may strike it rich who dares to play the Westing game.*

"Game? What game?" Turtle wanted to know.

"No matter," Judge Ford said, rising to leave. "This is either a cruel trick or the man was insane."

> FIFTH • *Sit down, Your Honor, and read the letter this brilliant young attorney will now hand over to you.*

It was uncanny. Several heads turned toward the coffin, but Westing's eyes were shut forever.

The brilliant young attorney fumbled through a stack of papers, felt his pockets, and finally found the letter in his briefcase.

"Aren't you going to open it?" Theo asked as the judge resumed her seat and put the sealed envelope in her purse.

"No need. Sam Westing could afford to buy a dozen certificates of sanity."

"The poor are crazy, the rich just eccentric," Mr. Hoo said bitterly.

"Are you implying, sir, that the medical profession is corrupt?" Denton Deere challenged.

"Shhh!"

> SIXTH • *Before you proceed to the game room there will be one minute of silent prayer for your good old Uncle Sam.*

Flora Baumbach was the only heir to cry. Crow was the only one to pray. By the time Sydelle Pulaski could assume a pose of reverence, the minute was up.

■ **THE WESTING GAME** ■

7

EIGHT CARD TABLES, each with two chairs, were arranged in the center of the game room. Sports equipment lined the walls. Hunting rifles, Ping-Pong paddles, billiard cues (a full rack, Turtle noticed), bows and arrows, darts, bats, racquets—all looked like possible murder weapons to the jittery heirs who were waiting to be told where to sit.

Theo wandered over to the chess table to admire the finely carved pieces. Someone had moved a white pawn. Okay, he'll play along. Theo defended the opening with a black knight.

On hearing Plum's throat-clearing signal, Sydelle Pulaski switched the painted crutch to her left armpit and flipped to a fresh page in her notebook. "Shhh!"

> SEVENTH • *And now, dear friends, relatives, and enemies, the Westing game begins.*
>
> *The rules are simple:*
> - Number of Players: 16, divided into 8 pairs.
> - Each pair will receive $10,000.
> - Each pair will receive one set of clues.
> - Forfeits: If any player drops out, the partner must leave the game. The pair must return the money. Absent pairs forfeit the $10,000; their clues will be held until the next session.
> - Players will be given two days' notice of the next session. Each pair may then give one answer.
> - Object of the game: to win.

"Did you hear that, Crow?" Otis Amber said excitedly. "Ten thousand dollars! Now aren't you glad I made you come, huh?"

"Shhh!" That was Turtle. The object of the game was to win, and she wanted to win.

> EIGHTH • *The heirs will now be paired. When called, go to the assigned table. Your name and position will be read as signed on the receipt.*
>
> *It will be up to the other players to discover who you really are.*

I • MADAME SUN LIN HOO, *cook*
    JAKE WEXLER, *standing or sitting when not lying down*

Grace Wexler did not understand her husband's joke about position. Mr. Hoo did, but he was in no mood for humor; ten thousand

dollars was at stake. Both pleaded for their absent spouses—
"Emergency operation," "My wife doesn't even speak English"—
to no avail. Table one remained empty and moneyless.

2 • TURTLE WEXLER, *witch*
    FLORA BAUMBACH, *dressmaker*

Sighs of relief greeted the naming of Turtle's partner, but Flora
Baumbach seemed pleased to be paired with the kicking witch.
At least, her face was still puckered in that elfin grin. Turtle had
hoped for one of the high-school seniors, especially Doug Hoo.

3 • CHRISTOS THEODORAKIS, *birdwatcher*
    D. DENTON DEERE, *intern, St. Joseph's Hospital, Department of Plastic Surgery*

Theo protested: He and his brother should be paired together;
Chris was his responsibility. Mrs. Wexler protested: Doctor D.
should be paired with his bride-to-be. D. Denton Deere protested,
but silently: If this had been arranged for free medical advice,
they (whoever they are) were mistaken. He was a busy man. He
was a doctor, not a nursemaid.

But Chris was delighted to be part of the outside world. He
would tell the intern about the person who limped into the
Westing house; maybe that was the murderer—unless his partner was the murderer! This was really exciting, even better than
television.

4 • ALEXANDER MCSOUTHERS, *doorman*
    J. J. FORD, *judge, Appellate Division of the State Supreme Court*

The heirs watched the jaunty doorman pull out a chair for the
judge. It had never occurred to them that Sandy was a nickname
for Alexander, but that couldn't be what Sam Westing meant by
It will be up to the other players to discover who you really are. Or
could it?

The judge did not return the chip-toothed smile. *Doorman,* he calls himself, and the others had signed simple things, too: *cook, dressmaker.* The podiatrist had even made fun of his "position." She must seem as pompous as that intern, putting on airs with that title. Well, she had worked hard to get where she was, why shouldn't she be proud of it? She was no token; her record was faultless. . . . Watch it, Josie-Jo. Westing's getting to you already and the game has barely begun.

5 • GRACE WINDSOR WEXLER, *heiress*
　　JAMES SHIN HOO, *restaurateur*

Grace Windsor Wexler ignored the snickers. If she was not the heiress now, she would be soon, what with her clues, Angela's clues, Turtle's clues, Denton's clues, and the clues of Mr. Hoo's obedient son. Five thousand dollars lost! Oh well, who needs Jake anyway? She'd win on her own. "You'll be happy to know that Mr. Westing was really my Uncle Sam," she whispered to her partner.

So what, thought Mr. Hoo. Five thousand dollars lost! He should have told his wife about this meeting, dragged her along. Sam Westing, the louse, has cheated him again. Whoever killed him deserves a medal.

6 • BERTHE ERICA CROW, *Good Salvation Soup Kitchen*
　　OTIS AMBER, *deliverer*

The delivery boy danced a merry jig; but Crow, her sore foot squeezed back into her tight shoe, headed for table six with a grim face. Why were they watching her? Did they think she killed Windy? Could the guilty know her guilt? Repent!

Crow limps, Chris Theodorakis noted.

7 • THEO THEODORAKIS, *brother*
　　DOUG HOO, *first in all-state high-school mile run*

They slapped hands, and Doug jogged to table seven. Theo moved more slowly. Passing the chessboard he saw that white had made a second move. He countered with a black pawn. Maybe he should not have written *brother,* but like it or not, that was his position in life. Chris was smiling at him in pure sweetness, which made Theo feel even guiltier about his resentment.

"I guess that makes us partners, Ms. Pulaski," Angela said.

"Pardon me, did you say something?"

8 • SYDELLE PULASKI, *secretary to the president*
   ANGELA WEXLER, *none*

Angela stepped tentatively behind the secretary, not knowing whether to ignore her disability or to take her arm. At least her crippled partner could not be the murderer, but it was embarrassing being paired with such a . . . no, she shouldn't feel that way. It was her mother who was upset (she could feel the indignant anger without having to look at Grace); her perfect daughter was paired with a freak.

What good luck, the hobbling Sydelle Pulaski thought. Now she would really be noticed with such a pretty young thing for a partner. They might even invite her to the wedding. She'd paint a crutch white with little pink nosegays.

Denton Deere was troubled. What in the world did Angela mean by "nun"?

■ ■ ■ ■ ■ ■ ■ ■ ■ ■ ■

Once again Edgar Jennings Plum cleared his throat.

"Nasal drip," Denton Deere whispered, confiding the latest diagnosis to his partner. Chris giggled. What's the crippled kid so happy about, the intern wondered.

> NINTH • *Money! Each pair in attendance will now receive a check for the sum of $10,000. The check can-*

not be cashed without the signatures of both partners.
Spend it wisely or go for broke. May God thy gold refine.

A piercing shriek suddenly reminded the Westing heirs of murder. While passing out the checks, the lawyer had stepped on Crow's sore foot.

"Is this legal, Judge?" Sandy asked.

"It is not only legal, Mr. McSouthers," Judge Ford replied, signing her name to the check and handing it to the doorman, "it is a shrewd way to keep everyone playing the game."

> TENTH • *Each pair in attendance will now receive an*
> *envelope containing a set of clues. No two sets of clues*
> *are alike. It is not what you have, it's what you don't*
> *have that counts.*

Placing the last of the envelopes on table eight, the young lawyer smiled at Angela. Sydelle Pulaski smiled back.

"This makes no sense," Denton Deere complained. Four clues typed on cut squares of Westing Superstrength Paper Towels lay on the table before him.

Arms and elbows at odds, with fingers fanned, Chris tried to rearrange the words in some grammatical, if not logical, order.

"Hey, watch it!" the intern shouted, as one clue wafted to the floor.

Flora Baumbach leaped from her chair at the next table, picked up the square of paper, and set it face down before the trembling youngster. "I didn't see it," she announced loudly. "I really didn't see it," she repeated under the questioning gaze of her partner, Turtle Wexler, *witch*.

The word she had seen was *plain*.

The players protected their clues more carefully now. Hunched over the tables, they moved the paper squares this way and that way, mumbling and grumbling. The murderer's name must be there, somewhere.

Only one pair had not yet seen their clues. At table eight Sydelle Pulaski placed one hand on the envelope, raised a finger to her lips, and tilted her head toward the other heirs. Just watch and listen, she meant.

She may be odd, but she's smart, Angela thought. Since each pair had a different set of clues, they would watch and listen for clues to their clues.

■ ■ ■ ■ ■ ■ ■ ■ ■ ■ ■

"He-he-he." The delivery boy slapped his partner on the back. "That's us, old pal: Queen Crow and King Amber."

"What's this: *on* or *no*?" Doug Hoo turned a clue upside down, then right side up again.

Theo jabbed an elbow in his ribs and turned to see if anyone had heard. Angela lowered her eyes in time.

J. J. Ford crumpled the clues in her fist and rose in anger. "I'm sorry, Mr. McSouthers. Playing a pawn in this foolish game is one thing, but to be insulted with minstrel show dialect . . ."

"Please, Judge, please don't quit on me," Sandy pleaded. "I'd have to give back all that money; it would break my wife's heart. And my poor kids. . . ."

Judge Ford regarded the desperate doorman without pity. So many had begged before her bench.

"Please, Judge. I lost my job, my pension. I can't fight no more. Don't quit just because of some nonsensical words."

Sticks and stones can break my bones, but words will never hurt me, she had chanted as a child. Words did hurt, but she was no longer a child. Nor a hanging judge. And there was always the chance . . . "All right, Mr. McSouthers, I'll stay." J. J. Ford sat down, her eyes sparking with wickedness. "And we'll play the game just as Sam Westing would have played it. Mean!"

Flora Baumbach squeezed her eyes together and screwed up her face. She was concentrating.

"Haven't you memorized them yet?" Turtle didn't like the way

Otis Amber's scrawny neck was swiveling high out of his collar. And what was Angela staring at?

"Yes, I think so," the dressmaker replied, "but I can't make heads or tails of them."

"They make perfect sense to me," Turtle said. One by one she put the clues in her mouth, chewed, and swallowed them.

∎ ∎ ∎ ∎ ∎ ∎ ∎ ∎ ∎ ∎ ∎

"Gibberish," Mr. Hoo muttered.

Grace Windsor Wexler agreed. "Excuse me, Mr. Plum, but what are these clues clues to? I mean, exactly what are we supposed to find?"

"Purple waves," Sandy joked with a wink at Turtle.

Mrs. Wexler uttered a cry of recognition and changed the order of two of her clues.

"It's still gibberish," Mr. Hoo complained.

Other players pressed the lawyer for more information. Ed Plum only shrugged.

"Then could you please give us copies of the will?"

"A copy will be on file . . ." Judge Ford began.

"I'm afraid not, Your Honor," the lawyer said. "The will not, I mean the will will will . . ." He paused and tried again. "The will will not be filed until the first of the year. My instructions specifically state that no heir is allowed to see any of the documents until the game is over."

No copy? That's not fair. But wait, they did have a copy. A shorthand copy!

Sydelle Pulaski had plenty of attention now. She smiled back at the friendly faces, revealing a lipstick stain on her front teeth.

"Isn't there some sort of a last statement?" Sandy asked Plum. "I mean, like the intern says, nothing makes any sense."

ELEVENTH ● *Senseless, you say? Death is senseless yet makes way for the living. Life, too, is senseless unless you know who you are, what you want, and which way the wind blows.*

So on with the game. The solution is simple if you know whom you are looking for. But heirs, beware! Be aware!

Some are not who they say they are, and some are not who they seem to be. Whoever you are, it's time to go home.

God bless you all and remember this:
Buy Westing Paper Products!

■ THE PAIRED HEIRS ■

8   DURING THE NIGHT Flora Baumbach's itsy-bitsy snowflings raged into a blizzard. The tenants of Sunset Towers awoke from clue-chasing, blood-dripping dreams, bound in twisted sheets and imprisoned by fifteen-foot snow-drifts.

No telephones. No electricity.

Snowbound with a murderer!

The slow procession looked like some ancient, mysterious rite as partner sought out partner on the windowless stairs, and silent pairs threaded through the corridors in the flickering light of crooked, color-striped candles (the product of Turtle's stint at summer camp).

"These handmade candles are both practical and romantic," she said, peddling her wares from apartment door to apartment door to frightened tenants at seven in the morning. (Oh, it's only Turtle.) "And the colored stripes tell time, which is very handy if your electric clock stopped. Each stripe burns exactly one-half hour, more or less. Twelve stripes, six hours."

"How much?"

"Not wishing to take advantage of this emergency, I've reduced the price to only five dollars each."

Outrageous. Even more so when the electricity came on two hours after her last sale. "Sorry, no refunds," Turtle said.

No matter. What was five dollars to heirs of an estate worth two hundred million? Clues, they had to work on those clues. Behind closed doors. Whisper, someone may be listening.

Not all the heirs were huddled in plotting, puzzle-solving pairs. Jake Wexler had retreated to his office after a long and loud argument with his wife. He sure could have used half of that ten thousand dollars, but he wouldn't admit it, not to her. The forfeited money upset her more than the murder of her uncle, if he was her uncle.

Five floors above, Jake's partner stood before the restaurant's front window staring at the froth on the angry lake, and beyond. No one had bothered to tell Madame Hoo about the Westing game.

Other players were snowbound elsewhere: Denton Deere in the hospital, Sandy at home. No one gave a thought to where Otis Amber or Crow might be.

But Sydelle Pulaski was there, thumping her crutch against the baseboards as she limped through the carpeted halls on the arm of her pretty partner. Not one, but seven tenants had invited her to morning coffee or afternoon tea (murderer or not, they had to see Pulaski's copy of that will).

"Three lumps, please. Angela drinks it black." Your health? "Thank the lord I'm still able to hobble about." Your job? "I was private secretary to the president of Schultz Sausages. Poor Mr. Schultz, I don't know how he'll manage without me." Your short-hand notes? "Thank you for the refreshments. I must hurry back for my medication. Come, Angela."

■ ■ ■ ■ ■ ■ ■ ■ ■ ■ ■

One heir had not invited them in, but that didn't stop Sydelle Pulaski from barging into apartment 2D. "Hi, Chris. Just thought we'd pop in to see how you're doing. Don't be scared. I'm not the murderer, Angela is not the murderer, and we don't think you are the murderer. Mind if I sit down?" The secretary toppled into a chair next to the invalid before he could reply. "Here, I stole a macaroon for you. It's so sticky you'll be tasting it all day; I must have six strands of coconut between my upper molars." Chris took the cookie. "Just look at that smile, it could break your heart."

Angela wished her partner had not said that; it seemed so insensitive, so crude. But at least Sydelle was talking to him, which was more than she was able to do. Angela, the fortunate one, standing like a dummy. "Um, I know Denton wants to work on the clues with you. He's snowbound, too."

"You ver-r pred-dy." How did "pretty" come out? He meant to say "nice." Chris bent his curly head over the geography book in his lap. She wasn't laughing at him. It was all right to ask her because she was going to marry his partner. "Wha ar-r g-gra-annz?"

Angela did not understand.

Chris fanned the pages of the book to a picture of a wheat field. "G-gra-annz."

"Oh, grains. You want to know the names of some grains. Let's see, there's wheat, rye, corn, barley, oats."

"O-ohss!" Angela thought the boy was going into a fit, but he was only repeating her last word: oats.

Sydelle was puffing her warm breath on the window and wiping a frosted area clean with her sleeve. "There, now you'll be able to watch the birds again. Anything else we can do for you, young man?"

Chris nodded. "Read m-me short-han n-noos."

The pretty lady and the funny lady moved quickly out the door. One limped, but it was a pretended limp (he could tell), not like the limper on the Westing house lawn.

Oats. Chris closed his eyes to picture the clues:

Grain = oats = Otis Amber. *For* + *d* (from *shed*) = Ford. But neither the delivery boy nor the judge limped, and he still hadn't figured out *she* or *plain*. He'd have to wait for Denton Deere; Denton Deere was smart; he was a doctor.

Chris raised his binoculars to the cliff. Windblown drifts buttressed the house—something moved on the second floor—a hand holding back the edge of a drape. Slowly the heavy drape fell back against the window. The Westing house was snowbound, too, and somebody was snowbound in it.

■ ■ ■ ■ ■ ■ ■ ■ ■ ■ ■

Only one of the players thought the clues told how the ten-thousand-dollar check was to be spent. *Take stock in America,* the will said. *Go for broke,* the will said.

"In the stock market," Turtle said. "And whoever makes the most money wins it all, the whole two hundred million dollars." Their clues:

SEA   MOUNTAIN   AM   O

stood for symbols of three corporations listed on the stock exchange: SEA, MT (the abbreviation for mountain), AMO.

"But *am* and *o* are separate clues," Flora Baumbach said.

"To confuse us."

"But what about the murderer? I thought we were supposed to find the name of the murderer?"

"To put us off the track." If the police suspected murder, she'd be in jail by now. Her fingerprints were over everything in the Westing house, including the corpse. "You don't really think one of us could have killed a living, breathing human being in cold blood, do you, Mrs. Baumbach? Do you?" Turtle did, but the dressmaker was a cream puff.

"Don't you look at me like that, Turtle Wexler! You know very well I could never think such a thing. I must have misunderstood. Oh my, I just wish Miss Pulaski had shown us her copy of the will."

Turtle returned to her calculations, multiplying numbers of shares times price, adding a broker's commission, trying to total the sums to the ten thousand dollars they had to spend.

Flora Baumbach may have been wrong about the murder, but she was not convinced of Turtle's plan. "What about *Buy Westing Paper Products?* I'm sure that was in the will."

"Great!" Turtle exclaimed. "We'll do just that, we'll add WPP to the list of stocks we're going to buy."

Flora Baumbach had watched enough television commercials to know that *Buy Westing Paper Products* meant that as soon as she could get to market, she'd buy all the Westing products on the shelf. Still, it felt good having a child around again. She'd play along, gladly. "You know, Turtle, you may be right about putting our money in the stock market. I remember the will said *May God thy gold refine.* That must be from the Bible."

"Shakespeare," Turtle replied. All quotations were either from the Bible or Shakespeare.

■ ■ ■ ■ ■ ■ ■ ■ ■ ■ ■ ■

Mr. Hoo moved aside a full ashtray with a show of distaste and rearranged the clues. "*Purple fruited* makes more sense."

Grace Wexler looked across the restaurant to the lone figure at the window. "Are you sure your wife doesn't understand English, I mean, after living here so long?"

"That's my second wife. She came over from Hong Kong two years ago."

"She does look young, but it's so hard to tell ages of people of the Oriental persuasion," Grace said. Why was he glaring at her like that? "Your wife is quite lovely, you know, so doll-like and inscrutable."

Hoo bit off half a chocolate bar. He had enough problems with the empty restaurant, a lazy son, and his nagging ulcer; now he had to put up with this bigot.

Grace lit another cigarette and rearranged the clues to read: *purple waves.* "You heard that doorman say 'purple waves'; it must mean something. And that ghastly secretary was wearing a dress with purple waves last night, not to mention her crutch."

"You should not speak unkindly of those less fortunate than you," Hoo said.

"You're quite right," Grace replied. "I thought the poor thing handled her infirmity with great courage—traveling mimosa, my future son-in-law says; he's a doctor, you know. Anyhow, Pulaski couldn't possibly be the murderer, not the way she gimps around. Besides, how could my Uncle Sam know she'd wear purple waves to his funeral?"

Hoo waved the cigarette smoke from his face. "The murderer had to have a motive. How about this: A niece murders her rich uncle to inherit his money?"

Good sport that she was, Grace tossed back her head and uttered an amused "Ha-ha-ha."

"Not that I care," Hoo said. "That cheating moneybags got what he deserved. What's the matter?"

"Look!" Grace pointed to the clues.

FRUITED   PURPLE   WAVES   FOR   SEA

"*For sea!* The murderer lives in apartment 4c!"

"I live in 4c," Hoo barked. "If Sam Westing wanted to say 4c he would have written number 4, letter C. S-e-a means *sea,* like what a turtle swims in."

"Come now, Mr. Hoo, we are both being silly. Have you spoken to your son about his clues?"

"Some son. If you can catch him, you can ask him." Hoo stuffed the rest of the candy bar in his mouth. "And some business I've got here. Everybody orders up, nobody orders down.

44

That coffee shop is sending me to the poorhouse. And your Angela and that Pulaski woman, they didn't show us the will, they didn't give us their clues, they didn't pay for three cups of jasmine tea and six almond cookies, and you smoke too much."

"And you eat too much." Grace threw her coin purse on the table and stormed out of the restaurant. Change, that's all he'll get from her; he'd have to beg on his knees before she'd sign Grace Windsor Wexler on the ten-thousand-dollar check, that madman. Some pair they made: Attila the Hun and Gracie the useless. Gracie Windkloppel Wexler, heir pretender, pretentious heir.

■ ■ ■ ■ ■ ■ ■ ■ ■ ■ ■

First, the money. They signed their names to the check; half would go into Doug Hoo's savings account; half would go to Theo's parents. Next, the clues:

HIS   N   ON   TO   THEE   FOR

"Maybe they're numbers: one, two, three, four," Theo guessed.

"I still say *on* is *no*," the bored track star said. He clasped his hands behind his head, leaned back in the coffee shop booth and stretched his long legs under the opposite bench. "And *no* is what we got: *no* real clues, *no* leads, *no* will."

After three cups of coffee, two pastries and a bowl of rice pudding with cream, Sydelle Pulaski had offered nothing in return.

Theo refused to give up. "Are you sure you didn't see anything unusual at the Westing house that night?"

"I didn't kill Westing, if that's what you mean, and the only unusual thing I saw was Turtle Wexler. I think the pest is madly in love with me; how's that for luck?"

"Get serious, Doug. One of the heirs is a murderer; we could all get killed."

"Just because somebody zapped the old man doesn't mean

45

he's going to kill again. Dad says . . ." Doug paused. His father's comment about awarding a medal to the murderer might be incriminating.

Theo tried another tack. "I was playing chess with somebody in the game room last night."

"Who?"

"That's what's strange; I don't know who. We'll have to find out which one of the heirs plays chess."

"Since when is chess-playing evidence for murder?"

"Well, it's something to go on," Theo replied. "And another thing: The will said no two sets of clues are alike. Maybe all the clues put together make one message, a message that points to the murderer. Somehow or other we'll have to get the heirs to pool the clues."

"Oh, sure. The killer can't wait to hand over the clues that will hang him." Doug rose. Snowbound or not, he had to stay in shape for the track meet. For the rest of the day he jogged through the hallways and up and down stairs, scaring the nervous tenants half out of their wits.

■ ■ ■ ■ ■ ■ ■ ■ ■ ■ ■

Judge J. J. Ford had no doubt that the clues she shared with the doorman were meant for her, but Sam Westing could toss off sharper insults than:

SKIES   AM   SHINING   BROTHER

His choice of words must have been limited; therefore, these clues were part of a longer statement. A statement that named a name. The name of the murderer.

No. Westing could not have been murdered. If his life had been threatened, if he had been in danger of any kind, he would have insisted on police protection. He owned the police; he owned the whole town. Sam Westing was not the type to let himself get killed. Not unless he was insane.

The judge opened the envelope given her by the incompetent Plum. A certificate of sanity, dated last week: "Having thoroughly examined . . . keen mind and memory . . . excellent physical condition . . . (signed) *Sidney Sikes, M.D.*"

Sikes. That sounded familiar. The judge scanned the obituary she had cut from Saturday's newspaper.

> . . . Samuel Westing and his friend, Dr. Sidney Sikes, were involved in a near-fatal automobile accident. Both men were hospitalized with severe injuries. Sikes resumed his Westingtown medical practice and the post of county coroner, but Westing disappeared from sight.

Sikes was Westing's friend (and, she remembered, a witness to the will), but he was also a physician in good standing. She would accept his opinion on Westing's sanity, for the time being at least.

Back to the clues. Look at her, the big-time judge, fussing over scraps of Westing Superstrength Paper Towels. "Forget the clues," she said aloud, rising from her desk to putter about the room.

Nibbling on a macaroon, she stacked the used coffee cups on a tray. If only that Pulaski person had let her study the will. That's where the real clues were buried, among the veiled threats and pompous promises, the slogans and silliness in that hodgepodge of a will.

In his will Sam Westing implied (he did not state, he implied) that (1) he was murdered, (2) the murderer was one of the heirs, (3) he alone knew the name of the murderer, and (4) the name of the murderer was the answer to the game.

The game: a tricky, divisive Westing game. No matter how much fear and suspicion he instilled in the players, Sam Westing knew that greed would keep them playing the game. Until the "murderer" was captured. And punished.

Sam Westing was not murdered, but one of his heirs was guilty—guilty of some offense against a relentless man. And that heir was in danger. From his grave Westing would stalk his enemy, and through his heirs he would wreak his revenge.

Which one? Which heir was the target of Westing's vindictiveness? In the name of justice she would have to find Westing's victim before the others did. She would have to learn everything she could about each one of the heirs. Who are they, and how did their lives touch Westing's, these sixteen strangers whose only connection with one another was Sunset Towers? Sunset Towers—she'd start from there.

Good, the telephones are working again. The number she dialed was answered on the first ring. "Hi there, this is a recording of yours truly, Barney Northrup. I'm at your service—soon as I get back in my office, that is. Just sing out your problem to old Barney here when you hear the beep." Beep.

J. J. Ford hung up without singing out her problem to old Barney. He, too, could be involved in Westing's plot.

The newspaper, she would try the newspaper; surely someone was snowbound there. After eight rings, a live voice answered. "We usually don't supply that kind of information over the phone, but since it's you, Judge Ford, I'll be happy to oblige. Just spell out the names and I'll call back if I find anything."

"Thank you, I'd appreciate that." It was a beginning. Sam Westing was dead, but maybe, just once, she could beat him at his own game. His last game.

■ ■ ■ ■ ■ ■ ■ ■ ■ ■ ■ ■

Having found what she wanted in Turtle's desk, Angela returned to her frilly bedroom where Sydelle Pulaski, glasses low on her nose, was perched on a ruffled stool at the vanity table, smearing blue shadow on her eyelids.

"First we tackle our own clues," the secretary said, frowning at the result in the threefold mirror. Unlucky from the day she was born, she now had a beautiful and well-loved partner. There was always the chance that they alone had been given the answer. She unsealed the envelope and held it out to Angela. "Take one."

Angela removed the first clue: *good*.

Now it was Sydelle's turn. "Glory be!" she exclaimed, thinking she had the name of the murderer. Her thumb was covering the letter *d*. The word was *hood*.

Angela's turn. The third clue was *from*.

Sydelle's turn. The fourth clue was *spacious*.

The fifth and last clue was—Angela uttered a low moan. Her hand shook as she passed the paper to her partner. The fifth and last clue was *grace*.

"Grace, that's your mother's name, isn't it?" Sydelle said. "Well, don't worry, that clue doesn't mean your mother is the murderer. The will says: *It is not what you have, it's what you don't have that counts.*" The secretary had not yet transcribed the shorthand, but she had read it through several times before hiding the notebook in a safe place. "By the way, are you really related to Mr. Westing?"

Angela shrugged. Sydelle assumed that meant no and turned to the clues.

GOOD   GRACE   FROM   HOOD   SPACIOUS

"The only thing I can figure from these clues is: *Good gracious from hood space.* As soon as the parking lot is shoveled out, we'll peek under the hoods of all the cars. A map or more clues may be hidden there. Maybe even the murder weapon. Now, let's hear about the other clues."

Angela reported on the clues gathered in the game room and during the day's comings and goings:

"*King, queen*. Otis Amber said, 'King Otis and Queen Crow.'

"*Purple waves*. Mother switched two clues around when Sandy mentioned those words.

"*On* (or *no*). Doug and Theo could not decide whether that clue was right side up or upside down.

"*Grains*. Chris Theodorakis thinks that clue refers to Otis Amber. You know, grains—oats.

"*MT*." Angela showed her partner the crumpled scrap of paper she had picked up along with Sydelle's dropped crutch during Flora Baumbach's tea party.

$$500 \text{ shares MT at } \$6 = \$3000$$
$$\text{broker's commission} = \underline{+90}$$
$$\$3090$$

"I checked Turtle's diary. She is not following any stock with a symbol like *MT*, so it must be one of her clues. *MT* could stand for either *mountain* or *empty*."

"Excellent," Sydelle Pulaski remarked. Her partner was beautiful, but not dumb. "Read all the clues together now."

GOOD   HOOD   FROM   SPACIOUS   GRACE
KING   QUEEN   PURPLE   WAVES
ON (NO)   GRAINS   MOUNTAIN (EMPTY)

Sydelle was disappointed. "*It is not what you have, it's what you don't have that counts.* And what we don't have is a verb. Nothing makes sense without a verb. What about the judge?"

"Judge Ford thought her clues were an insult, and she said something about playing a pawn in Westing's game. And she had a clipping of the obituary on her desk. This obituary." Angela handed Sydelle the newspaper taken from Turtle's drawer.

"What's that?"

It was a knock on the front door.

It was footsteps in the living room.

It was Theo. "Anyone for a game of chess?" he asked, leaning through the bedroom doorway.

"No, thank you," Sydelle replied, looking very busy.

Theo smiled shyly at Angela and left.

Sydelle read the obituary in Turtle's newspaper. The words *two hundred million dollars* were underlined, but she found a more interesting item. "Sam Westing was a master at chess; no wonder Theo's so interested. Do you know anything about the game, Angela?"

"A little," she replied slowly, putting the pieces in order. "The judge says she's a pawn and Otis Amber says he's the king, Crow's the queen— Oh well, it's probably just a coincidence."

"We can't leave any stone unturned," Sydelle insisted. "As the will says, *Object of the game: to win.*"

"What did you say?"

"Object of the game: to win."

"How about: object of the game: twin. Maybe the murderer is a twin."

"Twin!" Sydelle liked that. The only problem would be getting the murderer to admit that he (or she) is a twin. "Let's get back to my apartment. It's time I transcribed those notes."

Angela helped the invalid to her feet and nervously peered in both directions before stepping into the hallway.

Sydelle chuckled at her timidity. "There's nothing to be scared of, Angela. Westing was murdered for his money, and we're not rich yet. We won't be rich enough to be murdered until we find the name, and by the time we get the money from the estate, the murderer will be locked up in jail."

In spite of the impeccable logic, Angela looked back over her shoulder several times on the way to 3c.

"Strange." Sydelle stood before her open apartment door. She had slammed it shut on leaving, but had not locked the dead bolt; after all, not even a burglar could get into a snowbound building. Unless . . ."

Angela, too frightened to notice that Sydelle ran through the apartment with her crutch in the air, found her partner in the bathroom frantically tossing soiled towels from the hamper.

Sydelle Pulaski stared at the bare wicker bottom, then sank to the rim of the bathtub, shaking her head in disbelief. Someone in Sunset Towers had stolen the shorthand notebook.

■ LOST AND FOUND ■

9

EARLY THE NEXT morning a typed index card was tacked to the elevator's back wall:

■ ■ ■ ■ ■ ■ ■ ■ ■ ■ ■

> LOST: Important business papers of no value
> to anyone but the owner. Please return to
> Sydelle Pulaski, 3C. No questions asked.

■ ■ ■ ■ ■ ■ ■ ■ ■ ■ ■

The shorthand notebook was not returned, but the idea of a bulletin board was an instant success. By late afternoon the elevator was papered with notices and filled with tenants facing sideways and backwards, reading as they rode up and down.

■ ■ ■ ■ ■ ■ ■ ■ ■ ■ ■

> *Lost: Silver cross on filigree chain, topaz pin and*
> *earrings, gold-filled cuff links. Return to Grace Windsor*
> *Wexler, 3D. REWARD!*

■ ■ ■ ■ ■ ■ ■ ■ ■ ■ ■

All players willing to discuss sharing their clues come
to the coffee shop tomorrow 10 A.M.

■ ■ ■ ■ ■ ■ ■ ■ ■ ■ ■

WHOEVER STOLE MY MICKEY MOUSE CLOCK
BETTER GIVE IT BACK. JUST LEAVE IT IN
THE HALL IN FRONT OF APARTMENT 3D
WHEN NO ONE'S LOOKING.
TURTLE WEXLER

■ ■ ■ ■ ■ ■ ■ ■ ■ ■ ■

ORDER DOWN, NOT UP!
Or come on up to the fifth floor
and dine in elegance
at
SHIN HOO'S RESTAURANT
Specializing in exquisite Chinese cuisine.

■ ■ ■ ■ ■ ■ ■ ■ ■ ■ ■

LOST: STRING OF PEARLS. SENTIMENTAL VALUE. IF
FOUND, PLEASE BRING THEM TO APARTMENT 2C.
THANK YOU. FLORA BAUMBACH (DRESSMAKING
AND ALTERATIONS, REASONABLY PRICED)

■ ■ ■ ■ ■ ■ ■ ■ ■ ■ ■

FOUND: SIX CLUES
The following clues,
printed on squares of Westing Toilet Tissue,
were found in the third-floor hallway:
BRAIDED   KICKING   TORTOISE   'SI   A   BRAT

■ ■ ■ ■ ■ ■ ■ ■ ■ ■ ■

I am having an informal party this evening
from eight o'clock on. You are all invited.
Please come.

J. J. Ford, apartment 4D

■ ■ ■ ■ ■ ■ ■ ■ ■ ■ ■

Turtle, wherever you are—
Be home at seven-thirty SHARP!!!
Your loving mother

■ ■ ■ ■ ■ ■ ■ ■ ■ ■

"Mom, I'm home." No one else was.

On reading Mrs. Wexler's note in the elevator, Flora
Baumbach had insisted, "You must do what your mother says."
When Turtle replied, "Like showing her our clues?" Flora
Baumbach's answer was "Perhaps so. After all, she is your mother."

Flora Baumbach was sappy. Always smiling that dumb smile,
always so polite to everybody. And so timid. When they had
finally reached a snowbound broker, Flora Baumbach was so
nervous she dropped the telephone. Turtle had to admit to some
nervousness herself, but it was the first real order she had ever
placed. For a minute there, she thought she might choke on the
thumping heart that had jumped into her throat, but she had
pulled off the transaction like a pro. Now if only the stock market would go up, she'd show Mr. Westing about refining gold.
The next part of the will would read: "Whichsoever pair made
the most money with the ten thousand dollars inherits the whole
estate." She was sure of it.

"Oh, there you are." Grace Wexler acted as if Turtle was the
tardy one, but she quickly sweetened. "Come, dear, let's go to
your room and I'll fix your hair."

Her mother sat behind her on the edge of the narrow bed, loosed the dark brown hair, and brushed it to a gloss. She had not done that with such care in a long, long time.

"Have you eaten?"

"Mrs. Baumbach made me a dinner." Turtle felt the fingers dividing the hair into strands. Her mother was so warm, so close.

"Your poor father's probably starving; he's been so busy on the phone, changing appointments and all."

"Daddy's eating in the coffee shop; I just saw him there." Turtle had dashed in shouting: "The braided tortoise strikes again!" and kicked a surprised Theo in the shin. (It was Doug Hoo, not Theo, who had made the sign.)

Her mother twisted the three strands into a braid. "I think you should wear your party dress tonight; you look so pretty in pink."

Pretty? She had never used that word before, not about her. What's going on?

"You know, sweetheart, I'm rather hurt that you won't tell your own mother about your clues."

So that was it. She should have known. "My lips are sealed," Turtle said defiantly.

"Just one eensy-beensy clue?" Grace wheedled, winding a rubber band around the end of the braid.

"N-n-n," Turtle replied through sealed lips.

Angela came into the small room and tugged Turtle's braid (only her sister could get away with that).

Beaming on her favorite, Grace took her hand, then gasped. "Angela, where's your engagement ring?"

"I have a rash on my finger."

Thump, thump. Sydelle Pulaski appeared in the doorway. "Hi, what's everybody doing in the closet?"

"See, I told you this is a closet," Turtle said.

Grace ignored the complaint. It did no good being nice to that ungrateful child, never satisfied, always whining about something or other. "Oh, hello, Miss Pulaski."

"I've been feeling a bit weakly, thank you, but nothing can

keep me from a party." Sydelle's crutch was painted in black and white squares to match her black and white checkered dress. Her large hoop earrings were also black and white: the white one dangled from her left ear, the black from her right.

"The party is such a lovely idea," Grace said, warming up to the owner of the shorthand notes. "When I saw the invitation in the elevator I suggested to Mr. Hoo that he call the judge to see if she needed hors d'oeuvres; and sure enough, he got an order for six dozen." She turned to Angela. "Hadn't you better get dressed, dear? It's getting late. It's too bad Doctor D. can't escort you to the party, but your father and I will take you."

"Angela and I are going together; we're partners, you know." Sydelle had it all planned. They were to appear in identical costumes; tonight was the night they would discover if one of the heirs was a twin.

"I'm going to the party with Mrs. Baumbach," Turtle remarked. "The sign said everyone's invited."

Again Grace ignored her. "By the way, Miss Pulaski, I do hope you've changed your mind about showing me your notes."

It was the secretary's turn to seal her lips. She wouldn't put it past that uppity Grace Windsor Wexler to steal the notebook from an unfortunate cripple and then rub it in.

Grace tried again, her voice dripping with honey. "You know, of course, that if I do win the inheritance, everything I own goes to Angela."

Turtle bounded up. "Let me out of here: a person can't breathe in this closet." She kicked the bed, kicked the chair, kicked the desk, and elbowed past the disapproving secretary.

"What in the world is wrong with that child?" her mother said.

■ ■ ■ ■ ■ ■ ■ ■ ■ ■ ■

Judge Ford was instructing Theo in the art of bartending when the telephone rang. The snowbound newspaperman had found several items in the files.

"First, the engagement announcement of Angela Wexler to D. Denton Deere. Next, several clippings on a lawsuit brought against Sam Westing by an inventor named . . ."

"Hold on, please." Mr. Hoo waddled in with a large tray of appetizers. The judge pointed him to the serving buffet and apologized to her caller. "I'm sorry, would you repeat that name."

"James Hoo. He claimed Westing stole his idea of the disposable paper diaper."

"One minute, please." The judge cupped her hand over the mouthpiece. "Please don't leave, Mr. Hoo. I was hoping you'd stay for the party, as a guest, of course. Your wife and son, too."

Hoo grunted. He hated parties. He had seen his fill of people eating and drinking and acting like clowns, jabbering like . . . so that's it: jabbering, dropping clues. "I'll be right back."

The receiver hissed with an impatient sigh, then the researcher went on. "I've got a thick file of sports items on another Hoo, a Doug Hoo. Seems he runs a pretty fast mile for a high-school kid. That's all I could find on the names you gave me, but I still have stacks of Westing clippings to go through."

"Thank you so much."

The doorbell rang.

The party was about to begin.

■ THE LONG PARTY ■

10

"I HOPE WE'RE not too early." Grace Windsor Wexler always arrived at parties fashionably late, but not tonight. She didn't want to miss a thing, or a clue, or wait around in her apartment with a murderer on the loose. "I don't think you've met my husband, Doctor Wexler."

"Call me Jake."

"Hello, Jake," Judge Ford said. A firm handshake, laugh lines around his eyes. He needed a sense of humor with that social-climbing wife.

"What a lovely living room, so practically furnished," Grace commented. "Our apartments are identical in layout, but mine looks so different. You must come see what I've done with it. I'm a decorator, you know. Three bedrooms do seem rather spacious for a single woman."

What does she mean, three bedrooms? This is a one-bedroom apartment. "Would you care for an appetizer, Mrs. Wexler? I'm curious to know exactly how you are related to the Westing family."

The judge had hoped to take the "heiress" by surprise, but Grace gained time by coughing. "Goodness, that ginger is spicy—it's the Szechuan cooking style, you know. How am I related? Let me see, Uncle Sam was my father's oldest brother, or was he the youngest brother of my father's father?"

"Excuse me, I have to greet my other guests." The judge left the prattling pretender. Father's brother or father's father's brother, if the relationship was on the paternal side her maiden name would be Westing.

The party went on and on. No one dared be first to leave. (Safety in numbers, especially with a judge there.) So the guests ate and drank and jabbered; and they watched the other guests eat and drink and jabber. No one laughed.

"I guess murder isn't very funny," Jake Wexler said.

"Neither is money," Mr. Hoo replied glumly.

Deciding that his wife had found the perfect partner, the podiatrist moved on to the two women standing in silence at the front window. "Cheer up, Angie-pie, you'll see your Denton soon enough." His daughter twisted out of his embrace. "Are you all right, Angela?"

"I'm fine." She was not fine. Why did they ask about Denton all the time, as though she was nobody without him? Oh, it wasn't just that. It wasn't even the humiliation of her mother chiding her about the "twin" costume (in front of everybody) and sending her back to their apartment to change clothes. It was more than that, it was everything.

Jake turned to Madame Hoo. "Hi there, partner."

"She doesn't speak English, Dad," Angela said flatly.

"And she never will, Angela, if no one talks to her."

"Snow," said Madame Hoo.

Jake followed her pointing finger. "That's right, snow. Lots and lots of snow. Snow. Trees. Road. Lake Michigan."

"China," said Madame Hoo.

"China? Sure, why not," Jake replied. "China."

Angela left the chatting couple. Why couldn't she have made some sort of friendly gesture? Because she might do the wrong thing and annoy her mother. Angela-the-obedient-daughter did only what her mother told her to do.

"Hello, Angela. One of these tidbits might cheer you up." Judge Ford held the tray before her. "I hear you'll be getting married soon."

"Some people have all the luck," Sydelle Pulaski said, appearing from nowhere to lean over the tray to spear a cube of pork. "Of course, not all us women have opted for marriage, right, Judge Ford? Some of us prefer the professional life, though I must say, if a handsome young doctor like Denton Deere proposed to me, I might just change my mind. Too bad he doesn't happen to be twins."

"Excuse me." The judge moved away.

"I'm not having any luck at all, Angela," Sydelle whined. "If only your mother hadn't made you change clothes someone surely would have mentioned 'twin.' It's much harder to judge reactions when I have to bring up the subject myself. You shouldn't let your mother boss you like that; you're a grown woman, about to be married."

"Excuse me." Angela moved away.

"Yes, thank you, I would like a refill," Sydelle said to nobody and hobbled to the bar. "Something nonalcoholic, please, doctor's orders. Make it a double—twins."

Twins? What's she talking about, Theo wondered, staring at the black and white checkered costume. "Two ginger ales for the chessboard coming right up."

Hidden among her guests, the judge studied the two people standing off in the corner, the only pair in Sunset Towers who were not Westing heirs.

George Theodorakis placed his hand on the shoulder of his invalid son. A large, bronze, hard-working hand. Like Theo's. Theo resembled him in many ways: tall, wide shoulders, slim-waisted, the same thick, straight black hair; but age had chiseled the father's face into sharper planes. His troubled eyes stared across the room at Angela.

Catherine Theodorakis, a slight, careworn woman, gazed down on her younger son with tired, dark-circled eyes.

From his wheelchair Chris watched legs. Other than the funny lady with the shorthand notes, the only limpers were his brother Theo (Turtle had kicked him again) and Mrs. Wexler, who stood on one leg rubbing her stockinged foot against her calf. A high-heeled shoe stood alone on the carpet beneath her. Judge Ford didn't limp; besides, she couldn't be a murderer, in spite of his clues. *Nobody here looks like a murderer, they're all nice people, even this fat Chinese man who grumbles all the time.*

George Theodorakis greeted Mr. Hoo with "How's business?" Hoo spun around and stomped off from his fellow restaurant owner in a huff of anger.

James Hoo, inventor, that's who the judge wanted to talk to, but there was a problem at the bar. A long line had formed and it wasn't moving.

"There are sixteen white pieces and sixteen black pieces in chess," Theo was explaining to Sydelle Pulaski. "Do you play chess, Judge Ford?"

"A bit, but I haven't played in years." The judge led the secretary away from the crowded bar. *Theo must think the Westing game has something to do with chess. He may be right, it certainly is as complicated as a chess game.*

"But I did study," Doug was arguing.

The judge interrupted. "I haven't had a chance to thank you for the delicious food, Mr. Hoo. How long have you been in the restaurant business?"

"Running up and down stairs is not studying," Hoo said.

Sydelle Pulaski butted in. "Father and son? You look more like twins."

"You're equal partners with that Theodorakis kid," Hoo continued. "Why didn't you insist on holding the meeting in our restaurant instead of that greasy coffee shop?"

"Because some people don't like chow mein for breakfast," Sydelle Pulaski replied.

"There you are, dear." Grace patted a stray wisp of Angela's hair into place. "We must do something about your coiffure. I'll make an appointment for you with my hairdresser once the snow is cleared; long hair is too youthful for a woman about to be married. I can't understand what got into you, Angela, coming to this party in that old checkered dress and those awful accessories. Just because your partner dresses like a freak . . ."

"She's not a freak, Mother."

"I was just speaking to Mr. Hoo about catering the wedding shower on Saturday; I arranged for little Madame Hoo to serve in one of those slinky Chinese gowns. Where are you going? Angela!"

Angela rushed into Judge Ford's kitchen. She had to get away, she had to be alone, by herself, or she'd burst out crying.

She was not alone. Crow was there. The two women stared at each other in surprise, then turned away.

Poor baby. Crow wanted to reach out to the pretty child; she wanted to take her in her arms and say: "Poor, poor baby, go ahead and cry." But she couldn't. All she could say was "Here."

Angela took the dish towel from the cleaning woman and bunched it against her face to muffle the wrenching sobs.

The guests jabbered on and on about the weather, about food, about football, about chess, about twins. Turtle was slumped on the couch, scornful of dumb grown-up parties. You'd think one of them would know something about the stock market. She missed Sandy. Sandy was the only one in this dumb building she could talk to.

"Remember that quotation: *May God thy gold refine?*" Flora Baumbach asked. "Let's take a poll. I'll bet ten cents it's from the Bible."

"Shakespeare," Turtle argued, "and make it ten dollars."

"Oh my! Well, all right, ten dollars."

Together they made the rounds. Four votes for the Bible, three for Shakespeare, and one abstention (Madame Hoo did not understand the question).

Sydelle Pulaski voted for the Bobbsey twins. "And how do you know those words were in the will?" she asked suspiciously. Too suspiciously.

So that's what "Lost: Important business papers" meant. Somebody stole the shorthand notes. Turtle smiled at the delicious nastiness of it all. "I remember, that's all."

"If you remember so well, tell me what comes before that," Sydelle challenged.

"I don't know, what?"

The secretary had an audience now. "I don't mind telling you, but not if you ask like that."

Theo said, "Please?" not Turtle.

Sydelle turned toward him with what should have been a gracious manner, but she grimaced when the top of the crutch poked her in the chest. "The exact quotation," she announced loudly, hoping she was right, "is *Spend it wisely and may God thy gold refine.*"

Right or wrong, her guess was received with groans of disappointment. The heirs had expected more: a hint, a clue, something. It was time to go home.

11

A PALE SUN rose on the third snowbound morning. Lake Michigan lay calm, violet, now blue, but the tenants of Sunset Towers on waking turned to a different view. Lured by the Westing house, they stood at their side windows scoffing at the danger, daring to dream. Should they or shouldn't they share their clues? Well, they'd go to the meeting in the coffee shop just to see what the others intended to do.

Waiting in her closet of a room Turtle stared at the white-weighted branches of the maple on the hill. A twig snapped in silence, a flurry speckled the crusted snow. Sometimes when her mother was too busy to do her hair she sent Angela in, but today no one came. They had forgotten about her.

Brush and comb clutched in her fists like weapons, she stormed into apartment 2c. "Do you know how to braid hair?"

Flora Baumbach's pudgy fingers, swift with a needle, were clumsy with a comb, but after several tangled attempts she ended up with three equal strands. "My, what thick hair you have. I tried braiding my daughter's hair once, but it was too fine, soft and wispy like a baby's, even in her teens."

That was the last thing Turtle wanted to hear. "Was she pretty, your daughter?"

"All mothers think their children are beautiful. Rosalie was an exceptional child, they said, but she was the lovingest person that ever was."

"My mother doesn't think I'm beautiful."

"Of course, she does."

"My mother says I looked just like a turtle when I was a baby, sticking my head out of the blanket. I still look like a turtle, I guess, but I don't care. Where's your daughter now?"

"Gone." Flora Baumbach cleared the catch in her throat. "There, that braid should hold for the rest of the day. By the way, you've never told me your real name."

63

"Alice," Turtle replied, swinging her head before the mirror. Not one single hair escaped its tight bind. Mrs. Baumbach would make a good braider if only she'd stop yakking about her exceptional child. Rosalie, what a dumb name. "You'd better get to the meeting now. Remember, don't say a word to anyone about anything. Just listen."

"All right, Alice. I promise."

■ ■ ■ ■ ■ ■ ■ ■ ■ ■ ■

Theo wheeled his brother into the elevator and read the new message on the wall:

$25 REWARD for the return of a gold railroad watch inscribed: To Ezra Ford in appreciation of thirty years' service to the Milwaukee Road.
                              J. J. Ford, apartment 4D

"Fod-d-d, fo—de," Chris said.

"That's right, Judge Ford. Must be her father's watch. Probably lost it. I don't think it could have been stolen by anyone at the party last night."

Chris smiled. His brother had not understood him. Good. This might be an important discovery—Judge Ford's name was the same as her apartment number: Ford, 4D.

Theo led the waiting tenants through the kitchen where Mr. and Mrs. Theodorakis handed out cups of tea and coffee. "Sorry, we've run out of cream and lemons. Please help yourself to some homemade pastries."

Walking into the coffee shop was like entering a cave. A wall of snow pressed against the plate-glass window, scaling the door that once opened to the parking lot.

"I've got a car buried out there," Grace Wexler said, slipping into a booth opposite her partner. "Hope I find it before the snowplows do."

"If they ever get here," Mr. Hoo replied. "Good thing this meeting wasn't held in my restaurant, I'd go broke passing out free tea, if you call this tea." He held up a tea bag with contempt, then groaned on seeing his sweat-suited son jog in with a sweet roll between his teeth and vault over his hands onto a stool, "Where's your daughter the turtle?"

Grace Wexler looked around. "I don't know, maybe she's helping her father with his bookkeeping."

"Bookkeeping!" Mr. Hoo let out a whoop. Grace had no idea what was so funny, but she joined him in loud laughter. Nothing stirred people's envy more than a private joke.

Thinking she was being laughed at, Sydelle Pulaski dropped her polka dot crutch and spilled her coffee on Angela's tapestry bag before managing a solid perch on the counter stool.

Clink, clink. Theo tapped a spoon against a glass for attention. "Thank you for coming. When the meeting is over you are all welcome to stay for a chess tournament. Meanwhile, I'd like to explain why my partner and me . . . my partner and I . . . called this meeting. I don't know about your clues, but our clues don't make any sense." The heirs stared at him with blank faces, no one nodded, no one even blinked. "Now then, if no two sets of clues are alike, as the will says, that could mean that each set of clues is only part of one message. The more clues we put together, the better chance we have of finding the murderer and winning the game. Of course, the inheritance will be divided into equal shares."

Sydelle Pulaski raised her hand like a schoolgirl. "What about the clues that are in the will itself?"

"Yes, we'd appreciate having a copy of the will, Ms. Pulaski," Theo replied.

"Well, equal shares doesn't seem quite fair, since I'm the only one here who thought of taking notes." Sydelle turned to the group, one penciled eyebrow arched high over her red sequined spectacles.

Her self-congratulatory pose was too much for Mr. Hoo.

Grunting loudly, he squeezed out of the booth and slapped the shorthand pad on the counter.

"Thief!" the secretary shrieked, nearly toppling off the stool as she grabbed her notebook. "Thief!"

"I did not steal your notebook," the indignant Hoo explained. "I found it on a table in my restaurant this morning. You can believe me or not, I really don't care, because those notes you so selfishly dangled under our noses are completely worthless. My partner knows shorthand and she says your shorthand is nothing but senseless scrawls. Gibberish."

"Pure gibberish," Grace Wexler added. "Those are standard shorthand symbols all right, but they don't translate into words."

"Thief!" Sydelle cried, now accusing Mrs. Wexler. "Thief! Larcenist! Felon!"

"Don't, Sydelle," Angela said softly, her eyes set on the D she was embroidering.

"You wouldn't understand, Angela, you don't know what it's like to be. . . ." Her voice broke. She paused then lashed out at her enemies, all of them. "Who cares a fig about Sydelle Pulaski? Nobody, that's who. I'm no fool, you know. I knew I couldn't trust any one of you. You can't read my shorthand because I wrote in Polish."

Polish?!?!

■ ■ ■ ■ ■ ■ ■ ■ ■ ■ ■

When the meeting was again called to order Mr. Hoo suggested they offer Ms. Pulaski a slightly larger share of the inheritance in exchange for a transcript of the will—in English. "However, I repeat, neither my partner nor I stole the notes. And if anyone here suspects us of murder, forget it, we both have airtight alibis."

Doug choked on his sweet roll. If it got around to alibis, they'd find out where he was the night of the murder. On the Westing house lawn.

Mr. Hoo went on. "And to prove our innocence, my partner and I agree to share our clues."

"One minute, Mr. Hoo." Judge Ford stood. It was time for her to speak before matters got out of hand. "Let me remind you, all of you, that a person is innocent until proven guilty. We are free to choose whether or not to share our clues without any implication of guilt. I suggest we postpone any decision until we have given the matter careful thought, and until the time all of the heirs can attend. However, since we are assembled, I have a question to ask of the group; perhaps others do, too."

They all did. Wary of giving away game plans, the heirs decided the questions would be written out, but no names were to be signed. Doug collected the scraps of paper and handed them to Theo.

"Is anyone here a twin?" he read.

No one answered.

"What is Turtle's real name?" Doug Hoo was planning another nasty sign.

"Tabitha-Ruth," replied Mrs. Wexler with a bewildered look at Flora Baumbach, who said "Alice."

"Well, which is it?"

"Tabitha-Ruth Wexler. I should know, I'm her mother."

Doug changed his mind about the sign. He couldn't spell Tabitha-Ruth.

Theo unfolded the next question. "How many here have actually met Sam Westing?"

Grace Wexler raised her hand, lowered it, raised it halfway, then lowered it again, torn between her claim as Sam Westing's relative and being accused of murder. Mr. Hoo (an honest man) held up his hand and kept it up. His was the only one. Judge Ford did not think it necessary to respond to her own question.

Theo recognized the sprawling handwriting of the next question: "Who got kicked last week?" Chris did not receive an answer. The meeting was adjourned due to panic.

12

IT WAS SO sudden: the earsplitting bangs, the screams, the confusion. Theo and Doug ran into the kitchen; Mrs. Theodorakis ran out. Her hair, her face, her apron were splattered with dark dripping red.

"Blood," Sydelle Pulaski cried, clutching her heart.

"Don't just sit there," Catherine Theodorakis shouted, "somebody call the fire department."

Angela hurried to the pay phone on the wall and stood there trembling, not knowing whether to call or not. They were snowbound, the fire engines could not reach Sunset Towers.

Theo leaned through the kitchen doorway. "Everything's okay. There's no fire."

"Chris, honey, it's all right," Mrs. Theodorakis said, kneeling before the wheelchair. "It's all right, Chris, look! It's just tomato sauce."

Tomato sauce! Mrs. Theodorakis was covered with tomato sauce, not blood. The curious heirs now piled into the kitchen, except for Sydelle Pulaski, who slumped to the counter. She could have a heart attack and no one would notice.

Mr. Hoo surveyed the scene, trying to conceal his delight. "What a mess," he said. "That row of cans must have exploded from the heat of the stove." The entire kitchen was splattered with tomato sauce and soaked in foam from the fire extinguishers. "What a mess."

George Theodorakis regarded him with suspicion. "It was a bomb."

Catherine Theodorakis thought so, too. "There was hissing, then bang, bang, sparks flying all over the kitchen, red sparks, purple sparks."

"Cans of tomato sauce exploded," Doug Hoo said, defending his father. The others agreed. Mrs. Theodorakis was understandably hysterical. A bomb? Ridiculous. Sam Westing certainly did not appear to have been killed by a bomb.

Judge Ford suggested that the accident be reported to the police immediately in order to collect on the insurance.

"You might as well redecorate the entire kitchen," Grace Wexler, decorator, proposed. "It should be functional yet attractive, with lots of copper pots hanging from the ceiling."

"I don't think there's any real damage," Catherine Theodorakis replied, "but we'll have to close for a few days to clean up."

Mr. Hoo smiled. Angela offered to help.

"Angela, dear, you have a fitting this afternoon," Grace reminded her, "and we have so much to do for the wedding shower on Saturday."

In thumped Sydelle Pulaski. "I'm fine now, just a bit woozy. Goodness, what a nasty turn."

■ ■ ■ ■ ■ ■ ■ ■ ■ ■ ■

Having recovered from the nasty turn, Sydelle Pulaski settled down to transcribing her shorthand to Polish, then from Polish to English. Startled by loud banging on her apartment door, she struck the wrong typewriter key.

"Open up!"

Recognizing the voice, Angela unbolted the door to a furious Turtle. "All right, Angela, where is it?"

"What?"

"The newspaper you took from my desk."

Angela carefully dug through the embroidery, personal items, and other paraphernalia in her tapestry bag and pulled out the newspaper folded to the Westing obituary. "I'm sorry, Turtle. I would have asked for it, but you weren't around."

"You don't also happen to have my Mickey Mouse clock in there, too, do you?" Turtle softened on seeing her sister's hurt expression. "I'm only kidding. You left your engagement ring on the sink again. Better go get it before somebody steals that, too."

"Oh, I wouldn't worry about anyone stealing Angela's ring," Sydelle Pulaski remarked. "No mother would stoop that low."

The thought of Grace being the burglar was so funny to Turtle, she plopped down on the sofa and rolled about in laughter. It felt good to laugh; the stock market had fallen five points today.

"Angela, please tell your sister to get her dirty shoes off my couch. Tell her to sit up and act like a lady."

Turtle rose with a tongue click very much like her mother's, but she was not about to leave without striking back. Arms folded, she leaned against the wall and let them have it. "Mom thinks Angela was the one who stole the shorthand notebook." That got them. Look at those open mouths. "Because Mom asked to see it, and Angela does everything she says."

"Anyone could have stolen my notebook; I didn't double-lock my door that day." If Sydelle couldn't trust her own partner, she was alone, all alone.

"Did Mom really say that?" Angela asked.

"No, but I know how she thinks, I know what everybody thinks. Grown-ups are so obvious."

"Ridiculous," scoffed Sydelle.

"For instance, I know that Angela doesn't want to marry that sappy intern."

"Ridiculous. You're just jealous of your sister."

"Maybe," Turtle had to admit, "but I am what I am. I don't need a crutch to get attention." Oh, oh, she had gone too far.

"Turtle didn't mean it that way, Sydelle," Angela said quickly. "She used the word *crutch* as a symbol. She meant, you know, that people are so afraid of revealing their true selves, they have to hide behind some sort of prop."

"Oh, really?" Sydelle replied. "Then Turtle's crutch is her big mouth."

No, Angela thought, hurrying her sister out of the door and back to their apartment, Turtle's crutch is her braid.

■ ■ ■ ■ ■ ■ ■ ■ ■ ■ ■

The newspaperman called again to say he had found some photographs taken at Westingtown parties twenty years ago. "One of those names appears in a caption as Violet Westing's escort: George Theodorakis."

"Go on," the judge said.

"That's all." He promised to send her the clippings in the Westing file as soon as he was shoveled out.

The judge now knew of four heirs with Westing connections: James Hoo, the inventor; Theo's father; her partner, Sandy McSouthers, who had been fired from the Westing paper mill; and herself. But she had to learn more, much more about each one of the heirs if she hoped to protect the victim of Sam Westing's revenge.

She would have to hire a detective, a very private detective, who had not been associated with her in her practice or in the courts. J. J. Ford flipped through the Yellow Pages to *Investigators—Private.*

"Good grief!" Her finger stopped near the top of the list. Was it a coincidence or dumb luck? Or was she playing right into Sam Westing's hand? No choice but to chance it. The judge dialed the number and tapped her foot impatiently, waiting for an answer.

"Hello. If you're looking for a snowbound private investigator, you've got the right number."

Yes, she had the right number. It might be a trick, but it was no coincidence. The voices were one and the same.

■ **THE SECOND BOMB** ■

13   NO ONE WAS in the kitchen of Shin Hoo's Restaurant when the bomber set a tall can labeled "monosodium glutamate" behind similar cans on a shelf. The color-striped candle would burn down to the fuse at six-thirty;

whoever was working there would be at the other end of the room. No one would be hurt.

> *Due to the unfortunate damage to the coffee shop*
> **SHIN HOO'S RESTAURANT**
> *is prepared to satisfy all dinner accommodations.*
> *Order down, or ride up to the fifth floor.*
> *Treat your taste buds to a scrumptious meal*
> *while feasting your eyes on the stunning snowscape*
> *before it melts away. Reasonable prices, too.*

Grace Wexler tacked her sign to the elevator wall as she rode up to her new job. She was going to be the seating hostess.

"Where's the cook?" Mr. Hoo shouted (meaning his wife). He found Madame Hoo in their rear fourth-floor apartment kneeling before her bamboo trunk, fingering mementoes from her childhood in China. He hurried her up to the kitchen, too harried to find the words that would explain what was happening. Now where was that lazy son of his?

Doug jogged in from a tiring workout on the stairs. How was he supposed to know the restaurant would open early? Nobody bothered telling him.

"Some student you are; anyone with the brain of an anteater could have figured that out: people are short of food, the coffee shop is closed for repairs. Stop arguing, go take a shower, and put on your busboy outfit. Get moving!"

"Don't you think you're rather hard on the boy?" Grace commented.

"Somebody's got to give him a shove. If he had his way, he'd do nothing but run," Hoo replied between bites of chocolate. "You're not so easy on Angela, either."

"Angela? Angela was born good, the perfect child. As for the other one, well . . ."

"It's not easy being a parent," Hoo said woefully.

"You can say that again." Grace held her breath. Her husband would have done just that, said it again, but Mr. Hoo only nodded in shared sympathy. What a gentleman.

Only Mr. and Mrs. Theodorakis ordered down. The other tenants of Sunset Towers lined up at the reservations desk, waiting for Grace Windsor Wexler to lead the way. Oversized menus clutched in her arms, Grace felt the first proud stirrings of power rush up from her pedicured toes to the very top curl on her head. If Uncle Sam could pair off people, so could she.

"You see your brother every day, Chris, how about eating with someone else for a change?" She wheeled the boy to a window table without waiting for an answer. It would have been yes.

The two cripples together, Sydelle Pulaski thought. She'd show that high and mighty hostess, she'd show them all. She and Chris could have private jokes, too, and everybody would be sorry they weren't sitting with them.

"Whas moo g-goo g-gipn?" Chris asked, baffled by the strange words on the menu.

"I think it's boiled grasshopper." Sydelle screwed up her face and Chris laughed. "Or chocolate-covered moose."

"Frenssh-fry m-mouse," Chris offered. Now Sydelle laughed. They both laughed heartily, but no one envied them.

■ ■ ■ ■ ■ ■ ■ ■ ■ ■ ■

"Your brother seems to be enjoying Ms. Pulaski."

Theo nodded, awed by the beautiful Angela, three years older than he, so fair-skinned and blonde, so unattainable. Here he was sitting at the very same table with her, just the two of them, and he couldn't think of a single thing to say that wasn't stupid or childish or childishly stupid.

Usually the quiet one, Angela tried again. "Are you planning to go to college next year?"

Theo nodded, then shook his head. Say something, idiot. "I

got a scholarship to Madison, but I'm not going. I'm going to work instead." What big, worried sky-blue eyes. "The operation for Chris will be very expensive." That was worse, now she's feeling sorry for him. "If Chris had been born that way, maybe it wouldn't be so bad, but he was a perfectly normal kid, a great kid. And he's smart, too. About four years ago he started to get clumsy, just little things at first."

"Perhaps my fiancé can help." Angela bit her lip. Theo was not asking for charity. And *fiancé*, what an old-fashioned, silly word. "I went to college for a year. I wanted to be a doctor, but, well, we don't have as much money as my mother pretends. Dad said he could manage if that's what I really wanted, but my mother said it was too difficult for a woman to get into medical school." Why was she gabbing like this?

"I want to be a writer," Theo said. That really sounded like kid stuff. "Would you go back to college if you won the inheritance?"

Angela looked down. It was a question she did not want to answer. Or could not answer.

■ ■ ■ ■ ■ ■ ■ ■ ■ ■ ■ ■

Long before becoming a judge, Josie-Jo Ford had decided to stop smiling. Smiling without good reason was demeaning. A serious face put the smiler on the defensive, a rare smile put a nervous witness at ease. She now bestowed one of her rare smiles on the dressmaker. "I'm so glad we have this chance to become acquainted, Mrs. Baumbach. I had so little time to chat with my guests last night."

"It was a wonderful party."

Flora Baumbach appeared even smaller and rounder than she was as she sat twisting her napkin with hands accustomed to being busy. Was her face permanently creased from years of pleasing customers, or was a tragedy lurking behind that grin? "Have you always specialized in wedding gowns?"

"Mr. Baumbach and I had a shop for many years: Baumbach's for the Bride and Groom. Perhaps you've heard of it?"

"I'm afraid not." The judge would have said no in any case to keep her witness talking.

"Perhaps you've heard of Flora's Bridal Gowns? That's what I called my shop after my husband left. I don't know much about grooms' clothes, they're mostly rentals, anyway." Flora Baumbach lost her timidity; the judge let her chat away. "I'm using heirloom lace on the bodice of Angela's gown; it's been in my family for three generations. I wore it at my wedding, and I dreamed that someday I'd have a daughter who would wear it, too, but Rosalie didn't come along until I was in my forties, and . . ." The dressmaker stopped. Her lips tightened into an even wider grin. "Angela will make such a beautiful bride. Funny how she reminds me of her."

"Angela reminds you of your daughter?" the judge asked.

"Oh my, no. Angela reminds me of another young girl I made a wedding dress for: Violet Westing."

■ ■ ■ ■ ■ ■ ■ ■ ■ ■ ■ ■

The heavy charms on Sydelle Pulaski's bracelet clinked and clunked as she raised a full fork and flourished it in a practiced ritual before aiming it at her open mouth. Chris's movements were even jerkier. She's a good person, he thought, but she thinks too much about herself. Maybe she never had anybody to love.

"Here, let me help you to some of this delicious sweet and sour ostrich."

Their laughter drowned out the loud groan from another table where Turtle sat alone, a transistor radio plugged in her ear. The stock market had dropped another twelve points.

"I'm starved, let's sit down to eat." Head held high, Grace Wexler led her husband across the restaurant. "All I want is a corned beef sandwich, not a guided tour."

"Would you prefer to sit alone or with that young lady over there?"

"I thought I was going to sit with you."

"Please be seated," Grace replied. "Jimmy, I mean Mr. Hoo, will take your order shortly."

Jake snatched the menu from his wife and watched her glide (gracefully, he had to admit) to the reservations desk and whisper in Hoo's ear. (Jimmy, she calls him.) "That's a fine kettle of fish," he exclaimed, then turned to his dinner companion. "Fine kettle of fish. I'm so hungry even that sounds good, and from the looks of this menu that's probably what I'll get."

"I'm okay," Turtle replied, the final prices of actively traded stocks rumbling in her ear.

Mr. Hoo waddled over. "I recommend the striped bass."

"See, what did I tell you, a kettle of fish."

Turtle switched off the radio. She had heard enough bad news for one day.

"How about spareribs done to a crisp," Hoo suggested; then he lowered his voice. "What's the point spread on the Packers game?"

"See me later," Jake muttered.

"Go ahead and tell him, Daddy," Turtle said. "I know you're a bookie."

■ ■ ■ ■ ■ ■ ■ ■ ■ ■ ■ ■

"Can you stand on your legs?" Sydelle Pulaski asked. "Can you walk at all?"

People never asked Chris those questions; they whispered them to his parents behind his back. "N-n-no. Why?"

"What better disguise for a thief or a murderer than a wheelchair, the perfect alibi."

Chris enjoyed being taken for the criminal type. Now they really were friends. "When you ree m-m-me nos?"

"What? Oh, read you my notes. Soon, very soon." Sydelle

daintily touched the corners of her mouth with the napkin, pushed back her chair, and grabbed her polka-dot crutch. "That was a superb meal, I must give my compliments to the chef." She rose, knocking the chair to the floor, and clumped toward the kitchen door.

"Where is she going?" Angela, starting up to help her partner, was distracted by shouting in the corridor.

"Hello in there, anybody home?" Through the restaurant door came a bundled and booted figure. He danced an elephantine jig, stomping snow on the carpet, flung a long woolen scarf from his neck, and yelled, "Otis Amber is here, the roads are clear!"

That's when the bomb went off.

■ ■ ■ ■ ■ ■ ■ ■ ■ ■ ■

"Nobody move! Everybody stay where you are," Mr. Hoo shouted as he rushed into the sizzling, crackling kitchen.

"Just a little mishap," Grace Wexler explained, taking her command post in the middle of the restaurant. "Nothing to worry about. Eat up before your food gets cold."

A cluster of red sparks hissed through the swinging kitchen door, kissed the ceiling, and rained a shimmering shower down and around the petrified hostess. Fireflies of color faded into her honey-blonde hair and scattered into ash at her feet. "Nothing to worry about," she repeated hoarsely.

"Just celebrating the Chinese New Year," Otis Amber shouted, adding one of his he-he-he cackles.

Mr. Hoo leaned through the kitchen doorway, his shiny straight black hair (even shinier and straighter) plastered to his forehead, water dribbling down his moon-shaped face. "Call an ambulance, there's been a slight accident."

Angela dashed past Mr. Hoo into the kitchen. Jake Wexler made the emergency telephone call and sent Theo to the lobby to direct the ambulance attendants.

"Why are you standing there like a statue," Hoo shouted at his son.

"You told everybody to stay where they were," Doug said.

"You're not everybody!"

Madame Hoo tried to make the injured woman as comfortable as possible on the debris-strewn floor. Angela found the sequined spectacles, wiped off the wet, crystalline mess, and placed them on her partner's nose.

"Don't look so worried, Angela. I'm all right." Sydelle was in pain, but she wanted attention on her own terms, not as a hapless, foolish victim of fate.

"Looks like a fracture," an ambulance attendant said, feeling her right ankle. "Careful how you lift her."

The secretary suppressed a grunt. It was bad enough being drenched by the overhead sprinkler and draped with noodles; now they were carrying her right past them all.

Grace pulled Angela away from the stretcher. "You can visit your friend in a few days."

"Angela, Angela," Sydelle moaned. Pride or not, she wanted her partner at her side.

Angela stood between her determined mother and her distraught partner, paralyzed by the burden of choice.

"Go with your friend, Angie-pie," Jake Wexler said. Other voices chimed in. "Go with Pulaski."

Grace realized she had lost. "Perhaps you should go to the hospital, Angela; it's been so long since you've seen your Doctor D." She winked mischievously, but only Flora Baumbach smiled back.

■ ■ ■ ■ ■ ■ ■ ■ ■ ■ ■ ■

The policeman and the fire inspector visiting the scene agreed that it was nothing more than a gas explosion. Good thing the sprinkler system worked or Mr. Hoo might have had a good fire.

"What kind of a fire is a good fire," Hoo wanted to know.

"And what about the burglaries?" Grace Wexler asked.

"I'm with the bomb squad," the policeman explained. "You'll have to call the robbery detail for that."

"And what about the coffee shop accident?" Theo asked.

"Also a gas explosion."

Jake Wexler asked about the odds of having two explosions in two days in the same building.

"Nothing unusual," the fireman replied, "especially in weather like this, no ventilation, snow packed over the ducts." He instructed the tenants to air out their kitchens before lighting ovens.

Mrs. Wexler turned up the heat in her apartment and kept the windows open for the next three days. She did not want anything blowing up during Angela's party.

But the Wexler apartment was exactly where the bomber planned to set the next bomb.

■ PAIRS REPAIRED ■

14

THE SNOWPLOWS PLOWED and a warm sun finished the job of freeing the tenants of Sunset Towers (and the figure in the Westing house) from their wintry prisons.

Angela, disguised in her mother's old beaver coat and hat and in Turtle's red boots, was the first one out. Following Sydelle's instructions she hastily searched under the hood of every car in the parking lot. Nothing was there (nothing, that is, that didn't seem to belong to an automobile engine). So much for *Good gracious from hood space.*

Next came Flora Baumbach. Behind her a bootless Turtle tiptoed through puddles. Miracle of miracles: the rusty and battered Chevy started, but the dressmaker's luck went downhill from there. First, the hood of her car flew up in the middle of traffic. Then, after two hours of watching mysterious symbols move across the lighted panel high on the wall of the broker's office, her eyes began to cross. After three hours the grin faded from her face. "I'm getting dizzy," she said, shifting her position on the hard wooden folding chair, "and worse yet, I think I've got a splinter in my fanny."

"Look, there goes one of our stocks," Turtle replied.

SEA	GM	LVI	MGC	T	AMI	I
5$8½	5000$67	32¼		2$14 1000$65¼	3$19¼	8$22½

Flora Baumbach caught a glimpse of SEA 5$8½ as it was about to magically disappear off the left edge of the moving screen. "Oh my, I've forgotten what that means."

Turtle sighed. "It means five hundred shares of SEA was traded at $8.50 a share."

"What did we pay?"

"Never mind, just write down the prices of our stocks as they cross the tape like I'm doing. Once school opens it's all up to you." Turtle did not tell her partner that they had bought two hundred shares of SEA at $15.25 a share. On that stock alone they had a loss of $1,350, not counting commissions. It took nerves of steel to play the stock market.

■ ■ ■ ■ ■ ■ ■ ■ ■ ■ ■ ■

"The Mercedes is wiped clean and shiny like new," the doorman boasted. His face reddened around old scars as he rejected a folded five-dollar bill. "No tips, Judge, please, not after all you've done for the wife and me." The judge had given him the entire ten thousand dollars.

J. J. Ford pocketed the bill and, to make amends for her thoughtless gesture, asked the doorman about his family.

Sandy perched on the edge of a straight-backed chair, adjusted his round wire-framed glasses, repaired at the bridge with adhesive tape, across his broken nose, and told about his children. "Two boys still in high school, one daughter married and expecting my third grandchild (her husband just lost his job so they all moved in with us), another daughter who works part-time as a typist (she plays the piano real good), and two sons who work in a brewery."

"It must have been difficult supporting such a large family," the judge said.

"Not so bad. I picked up odd jobs here and there after I got fired from the Westing plant for trying to organize the union, but mostly I boxed. I wasn't no middleweight contender, but I wasn't bad, either. Got my face smashed up a few times too many, though; still get some pretty bad headaches and my brain gets sort of fuzzy. Some dummy of a partner you got stuck with, huh, Judge?"

"We'll do just fine, partner." Judge Ford's attempt at familiarity fell flat. "I did try to phone you, but your name was not listed."

"We don't have a phone no more; couldn't afford it with the kids making so many calls. But I did make some headway on our clues. Want to see?" Sandy removed a paper from the inside of his cap and placed it on the desk. Judge Ford noticed a flask protruding from the back pocket of his uniform, but his breath smelled of peppermint.

The clues as figured out by Alexander McSouthers:

SKIES AM SHINING BROTHER

SKIES—*Sikes* (Dr. Sikes witnessed the will)
AM BrothER—*Amber* (Otis Amber)
SHINing—*Shin* (the middle name of James Shin Hoo
or what Turtle kicks)
BROTHER—*Theo or Chris Theodorakis*

"Remarkable," the judge commented to Sandy's delight. "However, we are looking for one name, not six."

"Gee, Judge, I forgot," Sandy said dejectedly.

Judge Ford told him about Theo's proposal, but Sandy refused to go along. "It seems too easy, the clues adding up to one message, especially for a shrewd guy like Westing. Let's stick it out together, just the two of us. After all, I got me the smartest partner of them all."

Shallow flattery for the big tipper, the judge thought. McSouthers was not a stupid man; if only he was less obsequious—and less of a gossip.

The doorman scratched his head. "What I can't figure out, Judge, is why I'm one of the heirs. Unless Sam Westing just up and died, and there is no murderer. Unless Sam Westing is out to get somebody from his grave."

"I agree with you entirely, Mr. McSouthers. What we have to find out is who these sixteen heirs are, and which one, as you say, was Westing 'out to get.'"

Sandy beamed. They were going to play it his way.

■ ■ ■ ■ ■ ■ ■ ■ ■ ■ ■ ■

"What you need is an advertising campaign."

"What I need is my half of the ten thousand dollars."

"Five thousand dollars is what I estimate the redecorating and the newspaper ads will cost."

"Get out of here, get out!"

Grace stared at Hoo's smooth, broad face, at the devilish tufts of eyebrow so high above those flashing eyes, then she turned her back and walked out. Sometimes she wondered about that man—no, he couldn't be the murderer, he couldn't even kill the waterbug in the sink this morning. Grace spun around to see if she was being followed on the footstep-hushing carpet in the third-floor hall. No one was there, but she heard voices. They were coming from her kitchen. It was nothing, just Otis Amber shouting at Crow, something about losing their clues.

"I remember them, Otis," Crow replied in a soft voice. She felt strangely at peace. Just this morning she had been given the chance to hide her love in Angela's bag, the big tapestry shoulder bag she carries next to her heart. Now she must pray that the boy comes back.

"I remember them, too, that's not the point," Otis Amber argued. "What if somebody else finds them? Crow? Are you listening to me, Crow?"

No, but Grace Wexler was listening. "Really, Mr. Amber, can't you find another time to discuss your affairs with my cleaning woman. And where are you going, Crow?"

Crow was buttoned up in a black moth-eaten winter coat; a black shawl covered her head.

"It's freezing in here." Otis Amber shut the window.

Grace opened the window. "The last thing I need is a gas explosion," she said peevishly.

"Boom!" he replied. The two women were so startled that the delivery boy sneaked up on the unsuspecting for the rest of the week, shouting "Boom!"

Besides shouting "Boom!" Otis Amber delivered groceries from the shopping center to Sunset Towers, back and forth, to and fro. Not only did the tenants have to restock their bare shelves, they had to add Westing Paper Products by the gross to their orders. "Idiots, just because the will said *Buy Westing Paper Products*," he muttered, hefting a bulky bag from the compartment attached to his bike. Even Crow was using Westing Disposable Diapers to polish the silver and Westing Paper Towels to scrub the floors. (Is that what happened to their clues?) Poor Crow, she's taking this game harder than he had expected. She's been acting strange again.

"Boom!" Otis Amber shouted as the intern hurried by.

"Idiot," muttered Denton Deere.

Denton Deere paced the floor. "Listen, kid, I'd like to help you, but I'm only an intern specializing in plastic surgery. It would be different if you wanted a nose job or a face-lift." He had meant to be amusing; it sounded cruel.

Chris had not asked for charity. All he wanted was to play the game with the intern.

All the intern wanted was half of the ten thousand dollars. "I hear your brother suggested sharing clues. Sounds like a fine idea." No response. *Maybe the kid thinks I'm the murderer. The tenants must think so, the way they peered over their shoulders; and that delivery boy shouting like that. Why me? I'm a doctor; I took an oath to save lives, not take them.* "I'm a very busy man, Chris, I have lots of sick people depending on me. Oh well." Plowing his fingers through his stringy mouse-brown hair to keep it out of his eyes (*when would he find time for a haircut?*), he seated himself next to the wheelchair. "The clues are in my locker. What were they? 'The rain in Spain falls mainly on the plain'?"

"*F-for p-plain g-g-grain shed.*" Chris spoke slowly. He had practiced his recitation over and over, hour after lonely hour. "*G-grain*—oats—Otis Amber. *F-for, shed*—she, F-Ford. F-Ford lives in f-four D."

"Ford, apartment 4D, good thinking, Chris," The intern rose. "Is that all?"

Chris decided not to tell him about the limper on the lawn, not until the next time. His partner would have to visit him a next time, and a next time, as long as he didn't sign the check.

"Now, about signing the check," Denton Deere said.

Chris shook his head. No.

On a bench in the lobby Angela embroidered her trousseau, waiting for Denton. Dad had tried to teach her to drive, but she was too timid; he, too impatient. Why bother with driving lessons, her mother said, anyone as pretty as you can always find a handsome young man to chauffeur you. She should have insisted. She should have said no just once to her mother, just once. It was too late now.

Theo came in with an armload of books. "Hi, Angela. Hey, I found that quotation, or rather, the librarian found it. You know: *May God thy gold refine.*"

"Really?" Angela thought it unnecessary to remind him that it was Flora Baumbach and Turtle who had asked about the quotation, not her.

What lush lips, what white teeth, what fine and shiny hair. Theo fumbled between the pages of a chemistry book for the index card. On it was written the third verse of "America, the Beautiful":

> America! America!
> May God thy gold refine
> Till all success be nobleness
> And every gain divine.

Theo had begun reading the refrain and ended up singing. He shyly laughed off his foolishness. "I guess it doesn't have anything to do with money or the will, just Uncle Sam's patriotism popping up again."

"Thank you, Theo." Angela stuffed her embroidery in the tapestry bag on seeing Denton Deere rush off the elevator.

"Hello, Doctor Deere, how about a game of chess?"

"Let's go," the intern said, ignoring Theo.

Sandy opened the front door for the couple, whistling "America, the Beautiful." The doorman was a good whistler, thanks to his chipped front tooth.

"I can't drive you home; I'm on duty tonight."

"I'll take a cab."

"Why must you go back to the hospital? Your crazy partner isn't dying, you know."

"She's not crazy."

"She made up her so-called wasting disease, I call that crazy. Nothing was wrong with her legs until the explosion in the Chinese restaurant."

"You're wrong."

"First you ask me to look in on her, now you don't want my opinion. Anyhow, I called in a psychiatrist. Maybe you should talk to him, too. I've never seen you so troubled. What's wrong, the wedding dress isn't ready, the guest list is too long? You'll have to cope with more important matters than that once we're married. Unless you don't want to get married. Is that it?"

Angela twisted the engagement ring her mother made her wear in spite of the rash. No, she did not want to get married, not right away, but she couldn't say it, she couldn't tell him—them, not like that. Denton would be so hurt, her mother . . . the engagement was announced in the newspaper, the wedding gown, the shower . . . but once they found out she wasn't their perfect Angela . . .

How long has she been sitting here in the hospital corridor? A man in a business suit (the psychiatrist?) came out of Sydelle's room. "You must be Angela," he said. How had Sydelle described her—a pretty young thing? "I hear you're going to marry one of our interns." She was going to get married, her one claim to fame.

"How is Ms. Pulaski, Doctor?"

"Do you mean is she crazy? No. No more or less than anybody else in town."

"But the crippling disease, she made that up?"

"So what? The woman was lonely and wanted some attention, so she did something about it. And quite creatively, too. Those painted crutches are a touch of genius."

"Is that normal? I mean, it's not insane to shock people into noticing who you are?"

The doctor patted Angela's cheek as though she were a child. "No one was hurt by her little deception. Now, go in and say hello to your friend."

"Hello, Sydelle."

Without makeup, without jewelry, clothed only in a white hospital gown, she looked older, softer. She looked like a sad and homely human being. "You talk to the doctors?"

"It's a simple fracture," Angela replied.

"What else?" Sydelle turned her face to the wall.

"The doctor says your disease is incurable, but you could have a remission lasting five years, even more, if you take good care of yourself and don't overdo it."

"The doctor said that?" Maybe a few people could be trusted. "Did you bring my makeup? I must look a mess."

In the overstuffed tapestry bag, under Sydelle's cosmetic case, Angela found a letter. It was a strange letter, written in a tense and rigid hand:

> *Forgive me, my daughter. God bless you, my child.*
> *Delight in your love and the devil take doctor dear. Hast*
> *thou found me, O mine enemy? The time draws near.*

Taped at the bottom were two clues:

THY   BEAUTIFUL

■ **FACT AND GOSSIP** ■

15

FRIDAY WAS BACK to normal, if the actions of suspicious would-be heirs competing for a two-hundred-million-dollar prize could be considered normal.

At school, Theo studied, Doug Hoo ran, and Turtle was twice

sent to the principal's office for having been caught with a transistor radio plugged in her ear.

The coffee shop was full of diners.

Shin Hoo's restaurant had reopened, too, but no one came.

J. J. Ford presided at the bench, and Sandy McSouthers presided at the front door, whistling, chatting, collecting tidbits of gossip, and adding some of his own.

Flora Baumbach, her strained eyes shielded by dark glasses, drove Turtle to school on her way to the broker's office and picked her up in the late afternoon with a sheet of prices copied from the moving tape. They had lost $3,000 in five days.

"Paper losses," Turtle said. "Doesn't mean a thing. Besides, I didn't pick these stocks. Mr. Westing did."

Did he? The dressmaker thought of the clue Chris had dropped; no stock symbol had five letters or even resembled the word *plain*. But Flora Baumbach played fair and kept the secret to herself.

■ ■ ■ ■ ■ ■ ■ ■ ■ ■ ■ ■

Four people stood in the driveway's melting snow, shivering as the sun dropped behind Sunset Towers. The fifth jogged in place. No smoke had risen from the chimney since that fateful Halloween; still they stared up at the Westing house, murder on their minds.

"He looked too peaceful to have been murdered," Turtle said. She sneezed and Sandy handed her a Westing tissue.

"How would you know?" Doug replied. "How many people have you seen murdered?"

"Turtle's right," her friend Sandy said. "If Westing expected it, he'd have seen it coming. His face would have looked scared."

"Maybe he didn't see it coming," Theo argued. "The killer was very cunning, Westing said. I read a mystery once where the victim was allergic to bee stings and the murderer let a bee in through an open window."

"The window wasn't open," Turtle said, wiping her nose. "Besides, Westing would have heard the buzzing and jumped out of bed."

Doug had an idea. "Maybe the murderer injected bee venom in his veins."

Otis Amber flung his arms in the air. "Whoever said Sam Westing was allergic to bees?"

Doug tried again. "How about snake venom? Or poison? Doctors know lots of poisons that make it look like heart attacks."

Turtle almost kicked Doug, track meet or not. Her father was a doctor. She would not have minded if he had said "interns."

"I once heard about a murderer who stabbed his victim with an icicle," the doorman said. "It melted, leaving no trace of a murder weapon."

"That's a good one," Turtle exclaimed appreciatively.

Sandy had more. "Then there was a Roman who choked on a single goat hair someone put in his milk. And there was the Greek poet who was killed when an eagle dropped a tortoise on his bald head."

"Maybe Westing was just sleeping until Turtle stumbled and fell on his head," Doug suggested.

"That's not funny, Doug Hoo." How could she ever have had a crush on that disgusting jerk?

Doug would not let up. "And who was that suspicious person in red boots I saw opening the hoods of cars in the parking lot the other morning?" He looked at Turtle's booted feet.

"The thief stole my boots and put them back again. They leak."

"A likely story, Tabitha-Ruth." Doug pulled her braid and ran into the lobby at full speed.

Sandy placed a large hand on Turtle's shoulder, a comforting hand, and a restraining one.

Otis Amber hopped on his bike. "Can't stand around chitchatting about a murder that never happened. Sam Westing was a madman. Insane. Crazy as a bedbug." He pedaled off, shouting back, "We ain't murderers, none of us."

Theo could not agree. If there was no murderer, there was no answer; and without an answer, no one could win. "Sandy, did anybody leave Sunset Towers on Halloween night, before Turtle and Doug?"

The doorman scratched his head under his hat, thinking. "One day seems like the next, people coming and going. I can't remember."

"Try."

Sandy scratched harder. "Only ones I recall are Otis Amber and Crow. They left together about five o'clock."

"Thanks." Theo hurried into the building to check his clues.

Turtle had no reason to suspect Otis Amber or Crow or any of the heirs. Money was the answer. Her only problem was that dumb stock market; it didn't want to play the game. "Sandy, tell me another story."

"Okay, let's see. Once, long ago in the olden days, there was this soothsayer who predicted the day of his own death. That day came, and the soothsayer waited to die and waited some more, but nothing happened. He was so surprised and so happy to be alive that he laughed and laughed. Then, at one minute to midnight, he suddenly died. He died laughing."

"He died laughing," Turtle repeated thoughtfully. "That's profound, Sandy. That's very profound."

■ ■ ■ ■ ■ ■ ■ ■ ■ ■ ■

"Where's everybody?" The apartment was empty, as usual. Jake Wexler decided that Shin Hoo's was going to have a paying customer.

"I'd like a table, if you're not too crowded."

"I think I can squeeze you in," Hoo said, leading the podiatrist through the empty restaurant. "You must have liked those spareribs."

"Yeah, sure." Jake watched his wife slowly stack her papers at the reservations desk. At last, seeming to recognize him, she walked over. Jake returned his unlit cigar to his pocket (Grace hated the smell).

"I've already eaten," Grace said, sitting down.

"Hello to you, too," Jake replied.

He probably thinks that's funny. Since when do people go around saying hello to their husbands?

"What's new with you, Grace? Where are the kids? And what are all those presents doing on the coffee table? It's not your birthday and it's not our anniversary." What was she so upset about? "Or is it?"

"No, it isn't. Those are gifts for Angela, the wedding shower is tomorrow. Don't worry, you're not supposed to be there, just girls. The doorbell was ringing all morning, I couldn't leave the apartment for an instant; one at a time he delivered them, the smirking fool, and each time he shouted 'Boom!'"

She looked especially attractive today, Jake thought. Between the ringing doorbell and the booms, she had managed time for the beauty parlor and the sunlamp.

Mr. Hoo set the spareribs on the table and lowered himself to a chair.

Grace lost her scowl. "Since you're here, Jake, I'd like your opinion on the advertising campaign I'm planning. Jimmy and I are having a slight disagreement. I say that Shin Hoo's sounds like every other Chinese restaurant to English-speaking ears."

English-speaking ears? Jake bit his lip in an effort to keep silent.

"I say the restaurant needs a name people won't forget," Grace continued. "A name like Hoo's On First."

Jake could not help himself. He tried to cover a loud guffaw with louder coughing. Hoo pounded him on the back and apologized for the ginger.

"You remember that old baseball routine, Jake," Grace prompted.

Yes, he did. "Who's on second? No, What's on second; Who's on first."

"It's an idiotic name," Hoo argued. "Hoo's On First sounds like my restaurant is on First Street, or worse yet, on the first floor. Customers will end up in the coffee shop drinking dishwater tea."

"Not the way I'll promote it, they won't," Grace insisted. "Well, what's your opinion, Jake?"

The podiatrist put down the sparerib he was about to bite into. "Hoo's On First is a dandy name."

Before he could pick up the rib again, Hoo whisked the plate off the table. "Who elected you judge, anyhow?"

■ ■ ■ ■ ■ ■ ■ ■ ■ ■ ■ ■

The judge returned to Sunset Towers with clippings from the newspaper's files. Faithful Sandy was waiting.

Hoping to interrogate both George Theodorakis and James Shin Hoo, they alternated their dinner orders. One night they would order up, the next night they would order down. To their disappointment Theo delivered up. They had no questions to ask him, but he had one for the doorman.

"Chess?" Sandy replied. "Sorry, don't know the game. I'm a whiz at hearts, though. 'Shooter,' they call me."

Theo left them to their sandwiches and their work.

The private detective the judge had hired was still investigating the heirs, so tonight's project would be the Westing family.

Judge Ford opened the thin folder on Mrs. Westing. Mrs. Westing—no first name, no maiden name. In the few newspaper photographs in which she appeared, always with her husband, the captions read: Mr. and Mrs. Samuel W. Westing. A shadowy figure, a shy woman, she seemed to slip behind her husband before the camera clicked, or had her face masked by a floppy hat brim. A slim woman dressed in the fashion of the time: long, loose chemise, narrow shoes with sharply pointed toes and high spiked heels. A nervous woman, her hands, especially in the later pictures, were blurred. In the final photograph a black veil covered her face. She seemed to lean unsteadily against the stocky frame of her husband as they left the cemetery.

Sandy reported his findings. "Jimmy Hoo never met Mrs. Westing. Neither did Flora Baumbach. She says Violet's fiancé brought her to the shop for fittings. She says it's bad luck for a groom to see the bride in the wedding gown before the wedding; I guess she's right. Well, that's it. Nobody else admits to having known Mrs. Westing, except me."

"You knew her, Mr. McSouthers?" the judge asked.

"Well, not exactly, but I saw her once or twice." The doorman described Mrs. Westing as blonde, full-lipped, a good figure though on the skinny side. "Mostly I recall those full lips because she had a mole right here." He pointed to the right corner of his mouth.

Judge Ford did not remember a mole; she remembered copper-colored hair and thin lips, but it was so long ago, and well—Mrs. Westing was white. Very white.

Next, Westing's daughter. The judge studied the photograph under the headline:

VIOLET WESTING TO MARRY SENATOR

The senator turned out to be a state senator, a hack politician, now serving a five-year jail term for bribery. But Flora Baumbach was right about the resemblance. Violet Westing did look like Angela Wexler. And that was George Theodorakis, all right, dancing with her in the society page clippings.

"What does it all mean, Judge?" Sandy asked, squinting at the pictures through his smeared glasses. "Angela looks like Westing's daughter, and Theo looks like his father, the man Violet Westing really wanted to marry."

"How did you know that?"

Sandy shrugged. "It was common gossip at the time, that

Westing's daughter killed herself rather than have to marry that crooked politician. . . ."

Now the judge remembered; her mother had written her about the tragedy. "Tell me, Mr. McSouthers, you seem to know what's going on in this building: Is Angela Wexler involved with Theo in any way?"

"Oh no." Sandy was certain of that. "Angela and her intern seem happy enough with each other. At least, I hope so. I mean, if Sam Westing wanted to replay that terrible drama, Angela Wexler would have to die."

■ THE THIRD BOMB ■

16

"Boom!"

Grace Wexler slammed the door on the delivery boy's silly face and returned to her party with a pink-ribboned gift. The gossiping guests were sipping jasmine tea from Westing Paper Party Cups, nibbling on tidbits from Westing Paper Party Plates, and wiping their fingers on Westing Paper Party Napkins. Madame Hoo served in a tight-fitting silk gown slit high up her thigh, a costume as old-fashioned and impractical as bound feet. Women in China wore blouses and pants and jackets. That's what she would wear when she got home.

Grace clapped her hands for attention. "Girls, girls! It's time for the bride-to-be to open her presents. Angela, you sit here and everybody gather round."

Angela did as her mother said. She lowered herself to a cushion on the floor, ringed by gift boxes and surrounded by vaguely familiar faces. She had not invited her few friends from college; they were bent on careers, this wasn't their thing. These were her mother's friends and the newly married daughters of her mother's friends—and Turtle, who was leaning against the wall, arms folded, smirking. Lucky Turtle, the neglected child.

"Read it out loud, dear," Grace ordered, as Angela opened the card tied to the yellow-ribboned box.

> *To the bride-to-be in the kitchen stuck,*
> *An asparagus cooker and lots of luck.*
> from Cookie Barfspringer

"Thank you," Angela said, wondering which one was the Barfspringer.

The next gift was an egg poacher.

The box in pink ribbons contained another asparagus cooker.

"I sure hope Doctor Deere likes asparagus," someone remarked. The giver said she could return it for something else, although two might come in handy. "A doctor's wife has so much entertaining to do."

Angela glanced at her watch and reached for the tall, thin carton wrapped in gold foil.

"Look how Angela's hands are shaking; she's as nervous as a groom." Giggles. "Bride-to-be jitters." More giggles.

Slowly, Angela unknotted the gold ribbon. Carefully, she unfolded the gold foil. How neatly she did everything, the perfect child; not like Turtle, who ripped off wrappings, impatient to see what was inside.

"Hurry up, Angela, you're such a poke," Turtle complained. Suddenly there she was, kneeling down to peek under the lid.

"Get away!" Angela cried, jerking the gift up and away from her sister as the lid blasted off with a shattering bang. Bang! Bang! A rapid rat-a-tat-tat. Rockets shooting, fireballs bursting, comets shrieking, sparks sizzling. Two dozen framed flower prints falling off the wall.

Then it was over. Screams hushed to whimpers and the trembling guests crawled out from under tables and peered out of closets.

"Is anyone hurt?" Grace Wexler asked nervously. Other than

being scared out of ten years of their lives, thank you, they were fine. "Where's Angela?"

Angela was still seated on the cushion in the middle of the floor. Fragments of the scorched box lay in her burned hands. Blood oozed from an angry gash on her cheek and trickled down her beautiful face.

■ ■ ■ ■ ■ ■ ■ ■ ■ ■ ■ ■

Heirs, beware, Sam Westing had warned. They should have listened. Now it was too late.

The suspicious heirs gathered in the lobby around the police captain called in by Judge Ford. One of them was a murderer, they thought, and one of them was a bomber, and one of them was a thief. But which was which and who was who? Or could it be one and the same?

"Some game," Mr. Hoo grumbled, unwrapping a chocolate bar. One ulcer wasn't enough, Sam Westing had to give him three more. "Some game. The last one alive wins."

(Now, there's a likely suspect, Otis Amber thought. Hoo, the inventor; Hoo, the angry man, the madman.)

"The last one alive wins," Flora Baumbach repeated. "Oh my, what a terrible thing to say."

(Can't trust that dressmaker, Mr. Hoo thought. How come she's grinning at a time like this?)

The captain offered no help at all. "Neither the bomb squad nor the burglary detail has enough evidence to search the apartments," he explained.

"You call that justice?" Sandy asked.

(Good-natured Sandy couldn't be the one. He wasn't in the building when the first two bombs went off, or when the judge's watch was stolen, Jake Wexler thought. On the other hand, he sure did hate Sam Westing.)

"Yes, Mr. McSouthers, justice is exactly what I call it."

(Not her, not the judge, in spite of the clues, Chris thought. Unless she's one of those Black Panthers in disguise.)

"Those weren't gas explosions, those were bombs. Right?" Theo pressed the captain.

(A nice kid, that Theo. Doug, too, Flora Baumbach thought. But how often had she seen television interviews of next-door neighbors saying: Can't believe he killed thirteen people, he was such a nice kid. Oh my, oh my, what's gotten into me, thinking such a thing?)

The captain would not call them bombs. "More like childish pranks," he said.

(Childish pranks! That brat's capable of anything.)

Turtle stuck out her tongue at the sneering Doug Hoo.

"Evil pranks of the devil," Crow muttered. Her blessed Angela was almost killed.

"Crow could be the one. Bring hellfire down on all of us," Theo whispered to Chris, "but she wasn't in the building when the first two bombs went off."

"Yes, s-she was."

"No, she wasn't."

The captain described the so-called bombs. "Just a few fireworks triggered by a squat striped candle set in a tall open jar; the ribbon probably hid the air holes in the box. No one would have been hurt if the young lady had not tilted the box toward herself."

"A time bomb," Grace Wexler said, glaring at the person who delivered the gifts.

(An unhappy woman, that self-appointed heiress, the judge thought. Unfulfilled, possibly disturbed. Capable of the burglaries, perhaps, but not the bombings. She wouldn't have hurt her own daughter—at least, not Angela.)

"Don't look at me like that," Otis Amber shouted at Mrs. Wexler. "I don't own no striped candles, or no fireworks, neither."

(That idiot is the likeliest of all, Grace thought. But he wasn't around when the coffee shop blew up.)

"O-o-o-ggg a-a-ahh." The excitement was too much for Chris Theodorakis.

(That was one heir no one suspected. And Angela, of course, no one could suspect her.)

Otis Amber was not even sure of that. "Still waters run deep," he said. "He-he-he."

Turtle could not let him get away with that, even if it was true.

"Otis Amber limps," Chris noted the next day.

■ ■ ■ ■ ■ ■ ■ ■ ■ ■ ■

Her family kept reassuring her. "You're going to be fine, Angela, just fine."

The loud snore that erupted from the next hospital bed was Sydelle Pulaski pretending to be asleep.

"I still don't remember," Angela mumbled. Her bandaged cheek made speaking difficult. Her face hurt, her hands hurt—hurt very much.

"Traumatic amnesia," Jake Wexler said. "It happens after sudden accidents. Don't worry, Angie-pie, you're going to be fine."

"You're going to be fine, Angela, just fine," Grace said despondently. "I'll be back tomorrow. Come, Turtle."

"In a minute." Turtle waited for the door to close. She touched her sister's bandaged hand. "Thanks."

"For what?"

Another snore from Sydelle.

"Just thanks. The fireworks would have gone off in my face if you hadn't pulled the box toward you. Here, I brought your tapestry bag; I didn't look at your notes or clues, honest." But she had removed the incriminating evidence.

"Turtle, tell me the truth. How bad is it?"

"The doctor had to take some glass out of your hands, but no stitches. The burns will heal okay."

"And my face?"

"Some scarring, not bad really, Angela. Besides, you always said being pretty wasn't important, it's who you really are that counts."

Angela wondered about that. Maybe she was wrong. Maybe pretty was important. Maybe she was crazy, she must have been crazy.

"Don't worry, you'll still be pretty," Turtle said. "But, wow, that sure was a dumb thing to do."

Sydelle Pulaski's eyes popped open in surprise. Quickly she squeezed them shut and uttered another loud snore. Well, what do you know? Her sweet, saintly partner was the bomber. Good for her!

■ SOME SOLUTIONS ■

17 MONDAY WAS A gray, rainy day. Depressing. So was the stock market, which fell another six points. Turtle was jittery.

All the heirs were jittery. The bomb squad was called in several times to examine suspicious parcels. One turned out to be a sealed vacuum cleaner bag full of dust that Crow had set behind the incinerator door. Another was a box delivered to Mrs. Wexler. In it were bonbons (her favorite) and a note: *Love and kisses, Jake.*

"What do you mean, how come? Can't I send candy to my wife without getting the third degree? I thought you were looking on the thin side, okay?"

Grace made him eat the first piece.

The next day Grace received a larger box. In it the bomb squad found one dozen long-stemmed roses and a note: *For no reason at all, just love, Jake.*

The bomb squad was called again when Turtle ran after her partner through the lobby shouting "Mrs. BAUM-bach, Mrs. BAUM-bach!" Someone thought she had shouted "Bomb! Bomb!"

A hollow wind wailed through damp Tuesday. In the morning the stock market rose three points. "Bullish," said Flora Baumbach. In the afternoon the market dropped five points. "Bearish," said Flora Baumbach. Those were the only two trading terms she had learned.

Madame Hoo, a quicker student than the dressmaker, had learned more words: partner, money, house, tree, road, pots, pans, okay, football, good, rain, spareribs. Her teacher, Jake Wexler, visited her in the kitchen before he sat down to his daily lunch in the Chinese restaurant. Today his wife and Jimmy Hoo agreed to eat with their only customer on the promise that he would help them with their clues and not take a share of the inheritance if they won.

Grace laid their five words on the table.

"These are clues?" Jake looked down on *purple waves for fruited sea*. He switched two squares of Westing Superstrength Towels. "*Purple fruited* makes more sense. How about grapes or plums?"

Grace was about to insist on *purple waves,* but plums reminded her of something. "Plum," she said aloud. "Plum. Wasn't the lawyer's name Plum?"

"You're right, Grace," Mr. Hoo said excitedly. "You're absolutely right." He tore one of the clues in two: *fruit/ed*. "Ed Purple-fruit. Ed Plum!"

"We got it, we got it," Grace cried, leaping up to embrace her partner.

"I never did trust lawyers," Mr. Hoo shouted gleefully.

"What about the other clues: *for sea waves*?" Jake asked, but the happy, hugging and dancing, celebrating pair did not hear him.

"Boom!" said Madame Hoo, placing a plate of spareribs on the table. That word she had learned from Otis Amber.

■ ■ ■ ■ ■ ■ ■ ■ ■ ■ ■ ■

Sandy was proud of the notebook he bought, with its glossy cover photograph of a bald eagle in flight (sort of appropriate, he explained to the judge; fits in with Uncle Sam and all that). In it he painstakingly entered the information culled from reports the private detective delivered each day to Judge Ford's office: photostats of birth certificates, death notices, marriage licenses, drivers' licenses, vehicular accident reports, criminal records, hospital records, school records. To these the doorman added the results of his own snooping.

"My investigator is having a difficult time getting into the not-so-public records of Westingtown," the judge said. "We'll have to put the Westings aside and begin with the heirs."

"Since we're feasting on chicken with water chestnuts," Sandy said, "I'll start off with the Hoos." (Doug had delivered down.) He read aloud from his entry:

• HOO

JAMES SHIN HOO. Born: James Hoo in Chicago. Age: 50. Added Shin to his name when he went into the restaurant business because it sounded more Chinese. First wife died of cancer five years ago. Married again last year. Has one son: Douglas.

SUN LIN HOO. Age: 28. Born in China. Immigrated from Hong Kong two years ago. Gossip: James Hoo married her for her 100-year-old sauce.

DOUGLAS HOO (called Doug). Age: 18. High-school track star. Is competing in Saturday's track meet against college milers.

Westing connection: Hoo sued Sara Westing over the invention of the disposable paper diaper. Case never came to court (Westing disappeared). Settled with the company last year for $25,000. Thinks he was cheated. Latest invention: paper innersoles.

"I can take some credit for those paper innersoles," Sandy bragged. "My feet were killing me, standing at the door all day, so I said to Jimmy: 'Jimmy, if only somebody would invent a good innersole that didn't take up so much room like those foam-rubber things.' And sure enough, he did it. They're great, I got a pair in my shoes now, wanna see?"

"No, thank you." The judge was eating.

■ ■ ■ ■ ■ ■ ■ ■ ■ ■ ■ ■

It was past midnight when Theo finished his homework in the dim light of the study lamp. The wind was still howling, and something (a word? a phrase?) was still eluding him. He had been studying solutions in chemistry. Solutions—that was it! The solution is simple, the will said. He was sure of it.

By changing *for* and *thee* to the numbers *four* and *three*, Theo was able to arrange the clues into a formula (whether or not it was a chemical solution, let alone the Westing solution, was another matter).

$$N \quad H(IS) \quad FOR \quad NO \quad THEE \quad (TO) = NH^4NO^3$$

But four clue letters were left out: *isto, osit, itso, otis*. OTIS! He had it: a formula for an explosive, and the name of the murderer! He had to tell Doug.

"Where g-g-gogin?"

"Shhh!" Theo smoothed the blanket over his sleepy brother in the next bed, struggled into his bathrobe, and stumbled over the wheelchair as he tiptoed out of the room.

The elevator made too much noise, use the stairs. The cement was cold, he had forgotten his slippers. Two unmarked doors, which one? Tap, tap. Tap. A grunting voice, dragging footsteps. Please, let it be Doug, not Mr. Hoo or Judge Ford.

It was Crow. Clutching a robe about her gaunt frame, her unknotted hair hanging long and limp, she tried to focus her dulled eyes on the shocked face of her visitor. "Theo! Theo! The wind, I heard the wind. I knew you would come."

"Me?"

Grasping his hand, she pulled him into the maid's apartment between 4C and 4D and shut the door. "We are sinners, yet shall we be saved. Let us pray for deliverance, then you must go to your angel, take her away."

Theo found himself kneeling on the bare floor next to the praying Crow. He must be dreaming.

"Amen."

18

IT WAS FLORA Baumbach who braided Turtle's hair now, sometimes in three strands, sometimes four, sometimes twined with ribbons, while Turtle read *The Wall Street Journal*.

"Listen to this: 'The newly elected chairman of the board of Westing Paper Products Corporation, Julian R. Eastman, announced from London where he is conferring with European management that earnings from all divisions are expected to double in the next quarter.'"

"That's nice," Flora Baumbach said, not understanding a word of it.

Turtle gave the order for the day. "Listen carefully. As soon as you get to the broker's office I want you to sell AMO, sell SEA, sell MT, and put all the money into WPP. Okay?"

Oh my! That meant selling every stock mentioned in their clues and buying more shares of Westing Paper Products—at a loss of some thousands of dollars. "Whatever you say, Alice, you're the smart one."

Flora Baumbach's hands were gentle, they never hurried or pulled a stray hair. Flora Baumbach loved her, she could tell. "I like when you call me Alice," Turtle said, "but I better not call you Mrs. Baumbach anymore, because of the bomb scare, you know." Calling her Flora would spoil everything. "Maybe I could call you Mrs. Baba?"

"Why not just Baba?"

That's exactly what Turtle (Alice) wanted to hear. "Was your daughter, Rosalie, very smart, Baba?"

"My, no. You're the smartest child I ever met, a real business-woman."

Turtle glowed behind *The Wall Street Journal*. "I bet Rosalie baked bread and patched quilts and dumb stuff like that."

The dressmaker's sure fingers fumbled over the red ribbons she was weaving into a four-strand braid. "Rosalie was an exceptional child. The friendliest, lovingest . . ."

Turtle crumpled the newspaper. "Let's go. I'm late for school and you've got that big trade to make."

"But I haven't finished tying the ribbons."

"Never mind, I like them hanging." Turtle felt like kicking somebody, anybody, good and hard.

■ ■ ■ ■ ■ ■ ■ ■ ■ ■ ■

Sandy was not at the door when they left. He was in apartment 4D neatly writing in his patriotic notebook information gathered on the next heir.

● BAUMBACH

> FLORA BAUMBACH. Maiden name: Flora Miller. Age: 60. Dressmaker. Husband left her years ago, sends no money. She had a disabled child, Rosalie. Sold bridal shop last year after Rosalie died of pneumonia, age 19. Spends most of her time at the stockbrokers.
>
> *Westing connection:* Made wedding gown for Violet Westing, which she never got to wear.

Sandy turned to a fresh page, propped his feet on the judge's desk, and began to read the data supplied by the private investigator on Otis Amber. He laughed so hard he nearly fell off the tilting chair.

■ ■ ■ ■ ■ ■ ■ ■ ■ ■ ■

Haunted by last night's dream, Theo jogged behind his partner halfway to the high school before he uttered a breathless "Stop!"

Doug Hoo stopped.

"Who lives in the apartment next to yours?"

"Crow. Why?"

"Nothing." How come he didn't know that? Because no one ever wonders where a cleaning woman lives, that's why. But he wasn't like that, was he? Still, it must have been a dream. In the dream, the nightmare, Crow had given him a letter, but the only thing he found in his bathrobe pocket this morning was a Westing Paper Hankie. "Hey, wait!" Doug had started off again. "I figured out our clues. Ammonium nitrate. It's used in fertilizers, explosives, and rocket propellants."

"I knew those clues were a pile of fertilizer," Doug replied, jogging easily. Only one thing mattered: Saturday's big track meet. If he won or came in a fast second he'd have his pick of athletic scholarships. He didn't need the inheritance.

"Stand still and listen." Theo grabbed Doug by the shoulders and held him flat-footed to the ground. "Like it or not we're partners, and you've got to do your share."

"Sure," Doug replied. His father was angry, his partner was angry, and a bomber was blowing up Sunset Towers floor by floor. Some game! "What do you want me to do?"

"Follow Otis Amber."

■ ■ ■ ■ ■ ■ ■ ■ ■ ■ ■

Head tilted back, Flora Baumbach squirted drops in her eyes, blinked, and stared again at the moving tape.

HR	WPP	BRY	TA	Z	WPP
· 1000$42½	5000$39¼	27	5$17¼	5000$27¼	5000$39½

"Oh my!" Westing Paper Products had jumped four and a quarter, no, four and a half points. Her eyes must be blurry from the medicine. The dressmaker sat on the edge of her chair, biting her fingernails, waiting for WPP to cross the board again. There: WPP $40. Oh my, oh my! This morning she had paid thirty-five dollars a share. There it goes again: WPP $40¼. Oh my, oh my, oh my!

■ ■ ■ ■ ■ ■ ■ ■ ■ ■ ■

After classes, instead of running around the indoor track, Doug Hoo jogged out of the gym to the shopping center six blocks away. There was Otis Amber, placing two cake boxes in the compartment of his bike. He picked up a package from the butcher shop, and pedaled off, unaware of the sweat-suited figure trotting half a block behind him, and went into Sunset Towers to make his deliveries.

"Hi, Doug. Gonna run the mile under four minutes on Saturday?" the doorman asked.

"Sure hope so. Do me a favor, Sandy, give a loud whistle when Otis Amber comes out. Okay?"

Chip-toothed Sandy gave such a loud whistle that Otis Amber would have been deafened if the flaps of the aviator's helmet had not been snug against his ears.

Leaving his bicycle in the parking lot, Otis Amber boarded a bus. Doug ran the five uphill miles to a house with the placard: E. J. Plum, Attorney. He ran another three uphill miles after the bus that took the delivery boy to the hospital entrance.

Doug sank down in a waiting-room chair, wiped his face on his sweatshirt and picked up a magazine. Fascinated by the centerfold picture, he almost missed Otis Amber, who dashed out of the hospital as though fleeing for his life.

Hiding behind parked cars, Doug followed the delivery boy to another bus, ran four steep miles to a stockbroker's office (how is it that all roads go uphill?), from the broker to the high school, from the high school (downhill, at last) back to Sunset Towers.

The exhausted track star leaned against the side of the building, thankful he was not a long-distance runner.

"I gotcha!" Otis Amber poked a skinny finger into Doug's ribs. "He-he-he," he cackled, handing the startled runner a letter. "It's from that lawyer Plum. Says all the heirs gotta be at the Westing house this Saturday night. Sign here."

With his last ounce of energy he wrote *Doug Hoo, miler* on the receipt, then slid down the wall to a weary squat. Some miler. His feet were blistered; his muscles, sore; he could barely breathe, he might never run another step in his life.

■ ■ ■ ■ ■ ■ ■ ■ ■ ■ ■

On receiving the notice of the Westing house meeting, Judge Ford canceled her remaining appointments and hurried home. Time was running out.

Sandy read to her from his notebook:

● AMBER
OTIS JOSEPH AMBER. Age: 62. Delivery boy. Fourth-grade dropout. IQ: 50. Lives in the basement of Green's Grocery. A bachelor. No living relatives.
Westing connection: Delivered letters from E. J. Plum, Attorney, both times.

"I would've guessed Otis had an IQ of minus ten," Sandy said with a smile.

"Go on to the next heir," the judge replied.

● DEERE
D. DENTON DEERE. Age: 25. Graduate of UW Medical School. First-year intern, plastic surgery. Parents live in Racine (not heirs).

Westing connection: Engaged to Angela Wexler (see Wexlers), who looks like Sam Westing's daughter, Violet, who was also engaged to be married, but to a politician, not an intern.

"That's awful complicated, I know," the doorman apologized, "but it's the best I could do."

● PULASKI

SYDELLE PULASKI. Age: 50. Education: high school, one year secretarial school. Secretary to the president of Schultz Sausages. Is taking her first vacation in 25 years (six months' saved-up time). Lived with widowed mother and two aunts until she moved to Sunset Towers. Walked with a crutch even before she broke her ankle in the second bombing. Now needs two crutches (she paints them!).

Westing connection: ?

"We don't have any medical reports on her muscular ailment," Sandy reported. "The nurse at Schultz Sausages said she was in perfect health when she left on vacation."

"Strange," the judge remarked. A suspicious malady, no apparent Westing connection, somehow Sydelle Pulaski did not seem to fit in.

■ ■ ■ ■ ■ ■ ■ ■ ■ ■ ■

Sydelle Pulaski clasped the translated notes to her bosom. "My little secret, mustn't peek," she said coyly, but the doctors had come to see Angela.

The plastic surgeon loosed the tape from her check and peered under the gauze. "One graft should do it, but we can't operate until the tissue heals," he said to the intern, then spoke to the patient. "Call my secretary for an appointment in two months."

He strode out of the room, leaving Denton Deere to replace the bandage.

"I don't want plastic surgery," Angela mumbled. It still hurt to talk.

"Nothing to be frightened of. He's the best when it comes to facial repairs, that's why I brought him in."

"We'll have to postpone the wedding."

"We can have a small informal wedding."

"Mother wouldn't like that."

"How about you, Angela, what do you want?" He knew her unspoken answer was "I don't know."

The door flew open and slammed against the adjacent wall. "Where do you think you're going?" Denton pulled Turtle to a halt by one of the streaming ribbons twisted in her braid. "The sign says No Visitors."

"I'm not a visitor, I'm a sister. And get your germy hands off my hair."

Denton Deere hurried to seek first aid for his bleeding shin and sent the biggest male nurse on the floor to take care of Turtle, the same male nurse who chased Otis Amber out of the hospital for sneaking up on a nurse's aide carrying a specimen tray and shouting, "Boom!"

Turtle had time for one question. "Angela, what did you sign on the receipt this time after 'position'?"

"*Person.*"

"I changed mine to *victim*," Sydelle said.

Turtle paid no attention to the victim. She was more interested in the two men entering the room: the burly male nurse and that creep of a lawyer, Plum. "I gotta go. Don't say anything to anybody about anything, Angela, no matter what happens. Not even to a lawyer. You know nothing, you hear? Nothing!" She skirted Ed Plum, ducked under the outstretched hairy hands of the male nurse, slid down the hall, scampered down the stairs and out of the hospital.

"Hi, how are you?" Ed Plum smiled at Angela, ignoring the

patient in the other bed. He didn't recognize Ms. Pulaski without her painted crutch. "I'm sorry to hear about your accident. Otis Amber told me about it. Just thought I'd drop in for a chat." The young lawyer, who had admired the pretty heiress from the minute he first laid eyes on her, did not have a chance to chat.

Grace Wexler entered the room, saw the answer to the clues: Ed Purple-fruit, the murderer, standing over her daughter, and uttered a blood-curdling shriek.

■ ■ ■ ■ ■ ■ ■ ■ ■ ■ ■ ■

Three visitors in one day! The first was Otis Amber with a letter and another receipt to sign. Chris had pretended to be scared by the "Boom!" but he wasn't really. He had twitched because he was excited about going to the Westing house again, even if he hadn't figured out the clues.

Then Flora Baumbach came to see him. He wasn't nervous at all with that nice lady. She smiles that funny smile because she's sad inside. She once had a daughter named Rosalie. She told him how Rosalie would sit in the shop and say hello to the customers, and how she would feel the fabrics. Mrs. Baumbach made wedding dresses, which are mostly white, so she bought samples of materials with bright colors and patterns because Rosalie loved colors best. Rosalie had 573 different swatches in her collection before she died. Mrs. Baumbach said her daughter might have been an artist if things had turned out differently.

What would I have been if things had turned out differently?

The third visitor entered. Limping! His partner was limping! Too much excitement, his stupid body was jerking all over the place.

Denton Deere sat down next to the wheelchair. "Take it easy, Chris. Calm down, kid, I'm not the creature from the black lagoon, you know."

His partner, a doctor, watched horror movies on television, too. Slowly arms untangled, legs unsnarled. Slowly Chris stuttered out his news: Flora Baumbach felt so guilty about seeing their dropped clue that she told him one of her clues: *mountain.* "But we m-mus-n t-tell T-Turtle."

"Don't worry," the intern said, displaying a bruised shin.

Chris laughed, then stopped. "I s-sorry."

"*Mountain,* hmmm." Denton Deere thought about the new clue. "If a treasure is hidden in a grain shed on a mountain plain, I sure don't have time to look for it. Do you?"

"N-n-n."

"Let's forget the clues, I have something more important to tell you. Don't get excited, okay?"

Chris nodded. His partner was going to ask for the money.

Denton Deere stood. "I'll get your toothbrush and pajamas, then we'll go to the hospital. Don't get excited."

Chris got excited. How could he explain that what he wanted from his partner was companionship, not more probing, pricking doctors with their bad news that made his mother cry?

"Listen, Chris, can you hear me? Just overnight. I found a neurologist, a nerve doctor, who works on problems like yours."

"Op-p-pra-shn?"

"No operation. Did you hear me, Chris? No operation. The doctor thinks a new medicine may help, but he has to examine you, make some tests. I have your parents' permission, but no one will touch you unless we talk it over first, you and me, together. I promise."

Chris grimaced trying to smile. His partner said talk it over, the two of them, together. They were really partners now. "You c-c-cn have m-money."

"What? Oh, the money. Later. Here, let me take those, you won't need them in the hospital." Chris clung to his binoculars. "Well, I guess you do need them. Ready? Here we go!"

All of a sudden he was leaving Sunset Towers, pushed by his limping partner. Maybe Doctor Deere is not who and what he says he is. Maybe he is being kidnapped for ransom. Maybe he's being held hostage. Oh boy, he hasn't had so much fun in years.

19

THURSDAY WAS A sunny day, a glorious day; the autumn air was crisp and clear. None of the heirs noticed.

WPP crossed the tape at $44 . . . $44½ . . . $46. Forty-six dollars a share! Oh my! ("Don't sell until I give the word, Baba," Alice-Turtle had said.) Baba. The dressmaker smiled at her new name and eased back in the chair, but not for long. WPP $48¼. Oh my, oh my! Flora Baumbach bit her thumbnail to the quick. If only the child was here.

The child was being examined by the school nurse, having been caught again with a radio plugged in her ear. Turtle blamed her misbehavior on a toothache. "The only thing that soothes the horrendous pain is listening to music."

"You should see a dentist," the nurse said.

"I have an appointment next week," Turtle lied. "Can I go home now? The pain is truly unbearable."

"No." The nurse packed the tooth with foul-tasting cotton and sent her back to class. So every half hour Turtle had to ask permission to go to the lavatory in order to keep up with the latest stock market reports. "Bladder infection," she explained.

■ ■ ■ ■ ■ ■ ■ ■ ■ ■ ■

Crow polished Mrs. Wexler's silver teapot with a Westing Disposable Diaper for the third time. Two more days, the day after next. It was too painful, going back to that house, but Otis said she must, to collect her due. It was her penance to go back, not her due. Blessed is he who expects nothing.

"Boom! Just a warning to keep doors locked," the delivery boy said, dumping a carton of Westing Paper Products on the kitchen floor. "You know, Crow old pal, I think I figured out who the bomber is."

Crow stiffened as she stared at her distorted reflection in the shining silver. "Who?"

"That's right," Otis Amber said. "James Shin Hoo. He wanted to put the coffee shop out of business, right? Then he had to bomb his own restaurant so nobody would suspect him, right? And he catered the Wexler party. Nobody would notice if the caterer brought in an extra box along with the food, right?"

James Shin Hoo was the bomber. Crow's hands trembled, her face blotched with hate. That beautiful, innocent angel reborn; Sandy said her face will be scarred for life. James Shin Hoo, beware! Vengeance shall be mine.

■ ■ ■ ■ ■ ■ ■ ■ ■ ■ ■

The judge rearranged her docket in order to have these last days free. (Leave it to Sam Westing to interfere with her work.)

Sandy turned to his next entry. "It's an interesting one."

● CROW

BERTHE ERICA CROW. Age: 57. Mother died at childbirth, raised by father (deceased). Education: 1 year of high school. Married at 16, divorced at 40. Ex-husband's name: Windy Windkloppel. Hospital records: problems related to chronic alcoholism. Police record: 3 arrests for vagrancy. Gave up drinking when she took up religion. Started the Good Salvation Soup Kitchen on Skid Row. Works as cleaning woman in Sunset Towers, lives in maid's apartment on fourth floor. *Westing connection:* ?

"Yes, it is interesting," Judge Ford replied, "but it hardly tells us what we want to know."

■ ■ ■ ■ ■ ■ ■ ■ ■ ■ ■

"You've got a customer." Jake Wexler pointed a sparerib at the black-clad figure standing at the restaurant door.

"Must be a bill collector," Hoo said, frowning over his account book.

Grace looked up, saw it was only the cleaning woman, and returned to the sports photographs she was sorting. A dozen or more superstars would be framed and hung on one wall of Hoo's On First.

"Come on over and join us," Jake shouted.

Limping to their table, Crow heard Mrs. Wexler click her tongue. Sinful woman, she'll go to hell with her pride and her covetousness, and take that foot-butcher of a husband with her. And that one, the fat one, the glutton, the bomber, the mutilator of innocent children.

Maybe she is a customer, Hoo thought, recognizing the face clenched in righteous anger as that of a diner not being served fast enough. He rose and pulled out a chair for Crow. "My wife will be serving a Chinese tea lunch shortly."

Madame Hoo placed a variety of dumplings on the table, giggled at Jake, and ran back to the kitchen.

That tittering Madame Hoo was a beautiful woman. And quite young. Grace, casting a suspicious eye on her husband, was suddenly seized by a surge of gnawing jealousy (maybe it was just the fried dumpling).

Madame Hoo returned to pour the tea. Jake patted her hand. Good, Grace noticed, she's clutching her stomach, about time she felt jealous. The podiatrist turned his smile to Crow. "Nothing wrong with your appetite, I'm happy to see."

"Nothing is wrong with my mouth," the cleaning woman replied, looking down at her plate, "it's my feet that hurt. That corn you cut out didn't heal yet, I got a callus on the sole of my left foot, and my ingrown toenail is growing in again."

Grace clasped a hand over her mouth and ran out of the restaurant. Mr. Hoo headed for the kitchen.

"Your trouble comes from years of wearing the wrong kind of shoes," Jake lectured.

Crow wasn't listening. James Shin Hoo, the bomber, was coming back. He had something in his hand.

"Here, Crow, try these. I invented them myself. Paper innersoles. They'll make you feel like you're floating on air. It's tough standing on your feet all day. Here, take them."

Crow examined the two pads of spongy folded paper. "How much?"

"Nothing, compliments of the house."

Still suspicious, Crow slipped the innersoles into her shoes and tried walking. What a blessed relief. Otis Amber was wrong. James Shin Hoo was a charitable man, he couldn't be the bomber. Crow floated out of the restaurant without paying for her lunch.

■ ■ ■ ■ ■ ■ ■ ■ ■ ■ ■ ■

"Oh no, not another victim," Sydelle Pulaski cried, stuffing her notes under the mattress.

The nurse wheeled Chris next to Angela's bed and explained that the boy was being tested for a new medication. "Are you all right?" she asked, bending over the squirming patient.

Chris was trying to remove a blank, sealed envelope from his bathrobe pocket. He knew his brother had a crush on Angela. He figured Theo must have sneaked upstairs in the wrong bathrobe to slip this letter under Angela's door, then remembered she was in the hospital and was too shy to give it to her in person.

"Look at that smile," Sydelle exclaimed.

"F-from Theo," he said. Chris hoped to watch Angela read the love letter, but the nurse insisted he return to his room.

"Bye-bye, good luck," Sydelle called. Angela waved a bandaged hand.

"*M-moun-t-tain*," Chris replied. "From T-turtle." Serves her right for kicking his partner.

Mountain, Angela thought. Turtle's MT stood for *mountain,* not *empty.* And the letter was not from Theo.

> *Your love has 2, here are 2 for you.*
> *Take her away from this sin and hate*
> *NOW! Before it is too late.*

Again two clues were taped at the bottom:

WITH   MAJESTIES

"Crow and Otis Amber's clues are not *king* and *queen*," she told Sydelle. "They are *with thy beautiful majesties.*"

■ ■ ■ ■ ■ ■ ■ ■ ■ ■ ■

Sandy and the judge were still at work on the heirs.

● WEXLER

JAKE WEXLER. Age: 45. Podiatrist. Graduated from Marquette. Married 22 years, has two daughters (see below).

GRACE WINDSOR WEXLER. Born Gracie Windkloppel. Age: 42. Married to above. Claims to be an interior decorator. Spends most of her time in the Chinese restaurant or the beauty parlor. She and Jake (see above) have two daughters (see below).

ANGELA WEXLER. Age: 20. Engaged to marry D. Denton Deere (also an heir). One year college (high grades). Victim of third bombing. Embroiders a lot.

TURTLE WEXLER. Real name: Tabitha-Ruth Wexler. Age: 13. Junior-high-school student. Plays the stock market. Smart kid, but kicks people. Flora Baumbach calls her Alice.

Westing connection: Grace Windsor Wexler claims that Sam Westing is her real uncle. Angela looks like Violet Westing, so does Grace in a way, except she's older.

Sandy fidgeted with his pen. "There's something I didn't write down. Maybe I shouldn't tell you, you being a judge and all, but, well, Jake Wexler . . . he's a bookie."

No, he should not have told her. "A small-time operator, I'm sure, Mr. McSouthers," the judge replied coldly. "It can have no bearing on the matter before us. Sam Westing manipulated people, cheated workers, bribed officials, stole ideas, but Sam Westing never smoked or drank or placed a bet. Give me a bookie any day over such a fine, upstanding, clean-living man."

The doorman's face reddened. He pulled the dented flask from his hip pocket and downed several swigs.

She had been too harsh. "Would you like me to fix you a drink, Mr. McSouthers?"

"No thanks, Judge. I prefer my good old Scotch."

"Windkloppel!" The judge's outburst was so unexpected, Sandy had a hard time keeping down the last swig.

"Grace Wexler's maiden name is not Windsor, it's Windkloppel," the judge exclaimed, riffling through the pages of Sandy's notebook. "Here it is: 'Berthe Erica Crow. Ex-husband's name: Windy Windkloppel.'"

Sandy stopped coughing, started laughing. "Grace Windsor Wexler is related to somebody all right; she's related to the cleaning woman. Think she knows, Judge?"

"I doubt it. Besides, we cannot be certain of the relationship. I'd like to see the documents in Crow's folder again."

"I'm sure it's Windkloppel, Judge, I checked all my spellings three times over."

Judge Ford reread the private investigator's reports. "Mr. McSouthers, it is Windkloppel, but look carefully at the name of the woman in this interview."

Berthe Erica Crow? Sure I knew her. She
and her pa lived in the upstairs flat. We
were best friends, almost like sisters,
but she was the pretty one with her beautiful complexion and long gold-red hair.
She left school to marry a guy named
Windkloppel. Haven't seen or heard from
her since. She's not in any trouble, is she?

Transcript of a taped interview
with Sybil Pulaski, November 12.

"Pulaski!" the doorman said.

"Not just Pulaski," the judge pointed out. "*Sybil* Pulaski. Sam
Westing wanted Crow's childhood friend, Sybil Pulaski, to be
one of his heirs. He got Sydelle Pulaski instead."

"Gee, Judge, I never noticed that; boy, am I dumb. But what
does it mean?"

"What it means, Mr. McSouthers, is that Sam Westing made
his first mistake."

■ CONFESSIONS ■

20

FRIDAY CAME QUICKLY to the Westing heirs.
Too quickly. Time was running out.

Turtle skipped school. She was in trouble enough, but she
could build her own school and hire her own kind of teachers
once she became a millionaire.

In spite of having Turtle at her side, Flora Baumbach still stared
at the ever-changing, endless tape from the edge of the chair,
chewed what remained of her fingernails, and uttered an "Oh my!"
each time WPP went by. At two o'clock Westing Paper Products
sold at fifty-two dollars a share, its highest price in fifteen years.

"Now, Baba. SELL!"

■ ■ ■ ■ ■ ■ ■ ■ ■ ■ ■

Doug Hoo had a legitimate excuse from classes: tomorrow was the big track meet. He jogged, he sprinted, he ran at full speed—not on the track, but on the trail of Otis Amber. Back and forth from the shopping center to Sunset Towers, again and again and again and . . . hey, this is a new direction.

Otis Amber parked his delivery bike in front of a rooming house and went inside. Doug waited, hidden in a doorway across the street. And waited. People came and went, but no Otis Amber. Doug jogged up and down the block for two hours. Still no sign of Otis Amber.

Doug was cold and hungry, but at least his feet didn't hurt anymore. Last night when he asked Doc Wexler about the blisters, the podiatrist told him to see his father—his father, of all people. But those paper innersoles really worked.

At five o'clock Otis Amber skipped out of the rooming house, hopped on his bicycle, and returned to Sunset Towers empty-handed. Doug's assignment was over, well, almost over. Where was Theo?

■ ■ ■ ■ ■ ■ ■ ■ ■ ■ ■

Theo was being patched up in the hospital emergency room after a slight miscalculation in his "solution" experiment. Fortunately, no one else was around when the lab blew up.

"You like playing with explosives, kid?" the bomb squad detective asked. Accidents in high-school chemistry were not unusual, but this student lived in Sunset Towers.

"I was experimenting on chemical fertilizers," Theo replied, wincing as the doctor probed his shoulder for a glass shard.

"The first bomb went off in your folks' coffee shop, right? Your mother and father work you pretty hard, don't they?"

"They work harder than I do. Why all the questions? Your captain said the Sunset Towers explosions were just fireworks."

"Sure they were, but bombers have a funny habit of going in for bigger and bigger bangs. Until they get caught."

Theo had an alibi. He was nowhere near the Wexler apartment the day the third bomb went off. The detective grunted a warning about careless chemistry, but Theo had already learned his lesson. "Ouch!"

■ ■ ■ ■ ■ ■ ■ ■ ■ ■ ■ ■

At last the coffee shop owner himself delivered the up order. The judge came right to the point. "Mr. Theodorakis, tell me about your relationship with Violet Westing. I have reason to believe a life is in danger or I would not ask."

It was a question he had expected. "I grew up in Westingtown where my father was a factory foreman. Violet Westing and I were, what you'd call, childhood sweethearts. We planned to get married someday, when I could afford it, but her mother broke us up. She wanted Violet to marry somebody important."

The judge had to interrupt. "Her mother? Are you saying it was Mrs. Westing who arranged the marriage, not Sam Westing?"

George Theodorakis nodded. "That's right. Sam Westing tried to involve Violet in his business. I guess he hoped she'd take over the paper company one day; but she had her heart set on being a teacher. Besides, Violet didn't have much of a business sense. After that her father never paid her much attention."

"Go on." The judge held the witness in her stare.

The subject was becoming painful, and Mr. Theodorakis faltered several times in the telling. "Mrs. Westing handpicked that politician—probably figured the guy would end up in the White House and her daughter would be First Lady. But Violet thought he was nothing but a cheap political hack, a cheap crook. Violet was a gentle person, an only child. She couldn't turn against her mother, she couldn't face marrying that guy. . . . I guess she couldn't find any way out, except . . . Mrs. Westing sort of went off her rocker after Violet's death, and I . . . well, it was a long time ago."

"Thank you, Mr. Theodorakis," the judge said, ending the interrogation. The man had a different life now, different loves, different problems. "Thank you, you have been a big help."

Sandy was now able to complete the entry:

• THEODORAKIS

THEO THEODORAKIS. Age: 17. High-school senior. Works in family coffee shop. Wants to be a writer. Seems lonely; can't find anyone to play chess with.

CHRISTOS THEODORAKIS. Age: 15. Younger brother of above. Confined to wheelchair; disease struck about four years ago. Knows a lot about birds. *Westing connection:* Father was childhood sweetheart of Sam Westing's daughter (who looked like Angela Wexler). Mrs. Westing broke up the affair. She wanted daughter to marry somebody else, but Violet Westing killed herself before the wedding. Neither parents of above are heirs.

"I hear the new medicine they're trying out on Chris is doing some good," Sandy reported. "But the poor kid needs more help than medicine. He's real smart, you know. Chris could have a real future, be a scientist or a professor, even; but it will take a pile of money, more money than his folks could ever make, to put him through college with a handicap like that."

"The parents interest me more," the judge said. "Why are they not heirs?"

Sandy had some thought on that, too. "Maybe Sam Westing didn't want to embarrass George Theodorakis, him being married and all. Or maybe Westing figured he'd be too busy with his coffee shop to stay in the game. Or maybe Westing blamed him for his daughter's death, figuring they should have eloped."

"No, if Sam Westing blamed Mr. Theodorakis, he would have made him an heir in this miserable game," the judge replied. "There are too many maybe's here, which is what Sam Westing planned. We must not allow ourselves to be distracted from the real issue: Which heir did Sam Westing want punished?"

"The person who hurt him most?" Sandy guessed.

"And who would that be?"

"The person who caused his daughter's death?"

"Exactly, Mr. McSouthers. Sam Westing plotted against the person he held responsible for his daughter's suicide, the person who forced Violet Westing to marry a man she loathed."

"Mrs. Westing? But that's not possible, Judge. Mrs. Westing is not one of the heirs."

"I think she is, Mr. McSouthers. The former wife of Sam Westing *must* be one of the heirs. Mrs. Westing is the answer, and whoever she is, she is the one we have to protect."

■ THE FOURTH BOMB ■

21

THE DOOR TO apartment 2C opened. Flora Baumbach screamed, and Turtle flung herself on the pile of money they had been counting.

It was Theo, not the thief. "Can I borrow your bike for a few hours? It's very important." Theo was not a runner like Doug, who was fuming about his being so late. He needed the bicycle to follow Otis Amber, right now.

Turtle stared at him in stony silence.

"I didn't make that sign in the elevator; besides, you already kicked me for it. Please, Turtle." She still wouldn't answer, punk kid. "I had a long talk with the police today, but I refused to tell them who the bomber was."

"What's that supposed to mean?"

What does she think it means? It means that he and everybody else knows that Turtle is the bomber. "Never mind. Can I have your bike or not?"

"Why do you want it?"

Theo ground his teeth. Take it easy; anger won't help any more than blackmail did. Try being a good guy. "I saw Angela in the hospital today. She sends her regards."

"What's that supposed to mean?"

"You let me have that bike, Turtle Wexler, or—or else!"

Turtle did not have to ask what "or else" meant: police— bomber—Angela, but how did Theo find out? "Here!" She threw the padlock key across the room and waited for him to rush out before she let go of the money.

"He's such a nice boy," Flora Baumbach remarked.

"Sure," Turtle replied, dialing the telephone number of the hospital. "Angela Wexler, room 325."

"Room 325 is not accepting any calls."

Turtle hung up the phone. If Theo knew, others knew. Angela had set off those fireworks wanting to get caught, but it was different now. Now she was confused, now she was just plain scared. They could force a confession out of her in no time, the guilt was right there staring out of those big blue eyes. Maybe they're questioning her now. "Baba, I'm not feeling so good; I think I'll go home to bed."

■ ■ ■ ■ ■ ■ ■ ■ ■ ■ ■ ■

Weaving through rush-hour traffic on Turtle's bike, Theo trailed the bus to a seamy downtown district across the railroad tracks where Crow and Otis got off. Skid Row. The pair wandered through the dimly lit, littered, and stinking street, bending over grimy bums asleep in doorways, raising them to their unsteady feet, and leading the ragtag procession into a decaying storefront. Paint was peeling off the letters on the window: Good Salvation Soup Kitchen.

A drunken wreck of a man lurched into Theo, who put a quarter into the filthy outstretched hand, more out of fright than charity.

Snatches of hymn-singing drifted toward him as the last of the stragglers staggered through the door. Theo crossed the narrow street and pressed his nose against the steamy soup-kitchen window. Rows of wretched souls sat hunched on wooden benches. Crow stood before them in her neat black dress, her hands raised toward the crumbling ceiling. Behind her Otis Amber stirred a boiling mess in a big iron pot.

Theo pedaled back to Sunset Towers at a furious pace. Whatever brought Crow and Otis Amber to these lower depths was none of his business. He hated himself for spying. He hated Sam Westing and his dirty money and his dirty game. Theo felt as dirty as the derelicts he spied on. Dirtier.

■ ■ ■ ■ ■ ■ ■ ■ ■ ■ ■ ■

The judge thought they had finished with the heirs.

"Not quite," the doorman said.

• McSOUTHERS

ALEXANDER MCSOUTHERS. Called Sandy. Age: 65. Born: Edinburgh, Scotland. Immigrated to Wisconsin, age 3. Education: eighth grade. Jobs: mill worker, union organizer, prizefighter, doorman. Married, six children, two grandchildren.

Westing connection: Worked in Westing Paper plant 20 years. Fired by Sam Westing himself for trying to organize the workers. No pension.

Sandy turned to a blank page, pushed his taped glasses up the broken bridge of his nose, and looked at the judge. "Name?"

It had not seemed sporting to investigate one's own partner, but McSouthers was right, this was a Westing game. Of course, she had kept some facts from him about the other heirs, but only because she did not trust his blabbering. "Josie-Jo Ford, with a hyphen between Josie and Jo."

"Age?"

"Forty-two. Education: Columbia; law degree, Harvard." The judge waited for the doorman to enter the information in his slow, cramped lettering. He had to be meticulous in order to prove he was better than his eighth-grade education. It's a pity he had not gone further, he was quite a clever man.

"Jobs?"

"Assistant district attorney. Judge: family court, state supreme court, appellate division. *Appellate* has two *p*'s and two *l*'s. Never married, no children."

"Westing connection?"

The judge paused, then spoke so rapidly Sandy had to stop taking notes. "My mother was a servant in the Westing household, my father worked for the railroad and was the gardener on his days off."

"You mean you lived in the Westing house?" Sandy asked with obvious surprise. "You knew the Westings?"

"I barely saw Mrs. Westing. Violet was a few years younger than I, doll-like and delicate. She was not allowed to play with other children. Especially the skinny, long-legged, black daughter of the servants."

"Gee, you must have been lonely, Judge, having nobody to play with."

"I played with Sam Westing—chess. Hour after hour I sat staring down at that chessboard. He lectured me, he insulted me, and he won every game." The judge thought of their last game: She had been so excited about taking his queen, only to have the master checkmate her in the next move. Sam Westing had deliberately sacrificed his queen and she had fallen for it. "Stupid child, you can't have a brain in that frizzy head to make a move like that." Those were the last words he ever said to her.

The judge continued: "I was sent to boarding school when I was twelve. My parents visited me at school when they could, but I never set foot in the Westing house again, not until two weeks ago."

"Your folks must have really worked hard," Sandy said. "An education like that costs a fortune."

"Sam Westing paid for my education. He saw that I was accepted into the best schools, probably arranged for my first job, perhaps more, I don't know."

"That's the first decent thing I've heard about the old man."

"Hardly decent, Mr. McSouthers. It was to Sam Westing's advantage to have a judge in his debt. Needless to say, I have excused myself from every case remotely connected with Westing affairs."

"You're awfully hard on yourself, Judge. And on him. Maybe Westing paid for your education 'cause you were smart and needy, and you did all the rest by yourself."

"This is getting us nowhere, Mr. McSouthers. Just write: Westing connection: Education financed by Sam Westing. Debt never repaid."

■ ■ ■ ■ ■ ■ ■ ■ ■ ■ ■ ■

Theo, upset over his Skid Row snooping, took out his anger on the up button, poking it, jabbing it, until the elevator finally made its way down to the lobby. Slowly the door slid open. He stared down at the sparking, sputtering arsenal, yelled and belly-flopped to the carpet as rockets whizzed out of the elevator, inches above his head. Boom! Boom! A blinding flash of white fire streaked through the lobby, through the open entrance door, and burst into a chrysanthemum of color in the night sky. Then the elevator door closed.

The bomber had made one mistake. The last rocket blasted off when the elevator returned to the third floor. Boom!

By the time the bomb squad reached the scene (by way of the

stairs), the smoke had cleared, but the young girl was still huddled on the hallway floor, tears streaming down her turtle-like face.

"For heaven's sake, say something," her mother said. "Tell me where it hurts."

The pain was too great to be put into words. Five inches of Turtle's braid were badly singed.

Grace Wexler attacked the policeman. "Nothing but a childish prank, you said. Some childish prank; both my children cruelly injured, almost killed. Maybe now you'll do something, now that it's too late."

Unshaken by the mother's anger, the policeman held up the sign that had been taped to the elevator wall:

THE BOMBER STRIKES AGAIN!!!

On the reverse side was a handwritten composition: "How I Spent My Summer Vacation" by Turtle Wexler.

Grace grabbed the theme and shook it at her daughter, who was being rocked in Flora Baumbach's arms. "Somebody stole this from you, didn't they, Turtle? You couldn't have done such an awful thing, not to Angela, not to your own sister, could you Turtle? Could you?"

"I want to see a lawyer," Turtle replied.

■ ■ ■ ■ ■ ■ ■ ■ ■ ■ ■

The bomb squad, faced with six hours' overtime filling out forms and delivering the delinquent to a juvenile detention facility, decided it was best for all concerned to escort the prisoner to apartment 4D and place her in the custody of Judge Ford.

Judge Ford put on her black robe and seated herself behind the desk. Before her stood a downcast child looking very sad and very sorry. Not at all like the Turtle she knew. "You surprise me,

Turtle Wexler. I thought you were too smart to commit such a dangerous, destructive, and stupid act."

"Yes, ma'am."

"Why did you do it, Turtle? To hurt someone, to get even with someone?"

"No, ma'am."

Of course not. Turtle kicked shins, she was not the type to bottle up her anger. "You do understand that a child would not receive as harsh a penalty as an adult would? That there would be no permanent criminal record?"

"Yes, ma'am. I mean, no, ma'am."

She was protecting someone. She had set off the fireworks in the elevator to divert suspicion from the real bomber. But who was the real bomber? Nothing to do but drag it out of her, name by name, starting with the least likely. "Are you protecting Angela?"

"No!"

The judge was astounded by the excited response. Angela could not be the bomber, not that sweet, pretty thing. Thing? Is that how she regarded that young woman, as a thing? And what had she ever said to her except 'I hear you're getting married, Angela' or 'How pretty you look, Angela.' Had anyone asked about her ideas, her hopes, her plans? If I had been treated like that I'd have used dynamite, not fireworks; no, I would have just walked out and kept right on going. But Angela was different. "What a senseless thing to do," the judge said aloud.

"Yes, ma'am." Turtle stared down at the carpet, wondering if she had given Angela away.

Judge Ford rose and placed an arm around Turtle's bony shoulders. She had never wished for a sister until this moment. "Turtle, will you give me your word that you will never play with fireworks again?"

"Yes, ma'am."

"While we're at it, do you have anything else to confess?"

"Yes, ma'am. I was in the Westing house the night Mr. Westing died."

"Good lord, child, sit down and tell me."

Turtle began with the purple-waves story, went on to the whisperings, the bedded-down corpse, the dropped peanut butter and jelly sandwiches and her mother's cross, and ended with the twenty-four dollars she had won.

"Did either you or Doug Hoo call the police?"

"No, ma'am, we were too scared, we just ran. Is that a crime?"

The judge said it was a criminal offense to conceal a murder.

"But Mr. Westing didn't look murdered," Turtle argued. "He looked asleep, like he did in the coffin. He looked like a wax dummy."

"A wax dummy?"

Now Turtle was the one surprised by the excited response. The judge thinks it might have been a real wax dummy, not a corpse at all. Then what happened to Sam Westing?

The judge regained her composure. "Not reporting a dead body is a violation of the health code, but I wouldn't worry about it. Is there anything else, Turtle?"

"Yes, ma'am," Turtle replied, glancing at the portable bar. "Could I have a little bourbon?"

"What?"

"Just a little. On a piece of cotton to put in my cavity. My tooth hurts something awful."

Relieved at not having a juvenile alcoholic on her hands, Judge Ford prepared the home remedy. "Is that better? Good. You may go home now."

Home meant going to Baba. Baba loved her no matter what, and Turtle didn't care if the others thought she was the bomber—except Sandy. He was walking toward her right now, walking his bouncy walk, but not smiling. Sandy is disappointed in her, he thinks she hurt her own sister, he doesn't want to be friends anymore.

"How's my girl?" Sandy said, cupping his hand under her chin and lifting her head. "Whew! Hitting the bottle again?"

"It's just bourbon on cotton for my toothache."

"Yeah, I've heard that one before."

"Honest, Saaan-eee." Turtle was pointing inside her wide-open mouth.

The doorman peered in. "Wow, that's some cavity, it looks like the Grand Canyon. Tomorrow morning you're going to see my dentist—no back talk. He's very gentle, you won't feel a thing. Promise you'll go?"

Turtle nodded.

Sandy smiled. "Good, then down to business. My wife's having a birthday tomorrow. I thought one of your gorgeous striped candles would make a swell present."

"There's only one candle left," Turtle replied. "It's the best of the lot. Six super colors. I spent a lot of time making it; that's why I wouldn't part with it. But since it's for your wife's birthday, Sandy, I'll let you have it for only five dollars. And I won't charge you sales tax."

■ ■ ■ ■ ■ ■ ■ ■ ■ ■ ■

"Try not to stick your fanny out so far," Angela said from her chair. Now that Sydelle Pulaski depended on crutches, she lurched clumsily, hobbled by old habits.

"Just keep reading those clues." The secretary straightened, shoulders back, stomach in, until her next step.

With their telephone switched off and Contagious Disease added to the No Visitors sign, the bomb victims had privacy at last. Sydelle had twice read the entire will aloud. Now Angela, her hands unbandaged, was reshuffling the collected clues.

GRAINS   SPACIOUS   GRACE   GOOD   HOOD
WITH   BEAUTIFUL   MAJESTIES   FROM   THY   PURPLE
WAVES   ON(NO)   MOUNTAIN

"Again," Sydelle ordered. "Change them around and read either the word *on* or the word *no;* both together are confusing."

> GOOD   SPACIOUS   GRAINS   WITH   GRACE
> ON   THY   PURPLE   MOUNTAIN   HOOD   WAVES
> FROM   MAJESTIES   BEAUTIFUL

"Shh!" Someone was at the door. Angela picked up the note that was slipped underneath.

> *My darling Angela: I guess the sign on the door*
> *means I should stay away, too. I understand. We*
> *both need time to think things over. I'll wait. I love*
> *you—Denton*

"What does it say, what does it say?" Sydelle pressed, but Angela read only the postscript aloud:

> P.S. *You have another admirer. Chris wants to give*
> *you and Ms. Pulaski one of our clues. (Flora*
> *Baumbach has seen it, too.) The word is* plain.

"Like an airplane?" Sydelle asked.

"No, plain, like ordinary. Like the wide open plains."

"Plains, grains. Quick, Angela, read the clues again."

> GOOD   HOOD   FROM   SPACIOUS   PLAIN
> GRAINS   ON   WITH   BEAUTIFUL   WAVES
> GRACE   THY   PURPLE   MOUNTAIN   MAJESTIES

"That's it, Angela. We got it, we got it!" Sydelle could barely control her excitement. "The will said, *Sing in praise of this gen-*

erous land. The will said, *May God thy gold refine*. America, Angela, America! *Purple mountain majesties,* Angela. Whoopee!"

Fortunately Sydelle Pulaski was close to the bed when she threw her crutches in the air.

22

SATURDAY MORNING, a new message was posted in the elevator:

> I, TURTLE WEXLER, CONFESS TO THOSE
> FOUR BOMBS. I'M SORRY, IT WAS A DUMB
> THING TO DO AND I WON'T DO IT AGAIN.
> BUT! I AM NOT THE BURGLAR AND I NEVER
> MURDERED ANYBODY, EVER.
>
> YOUR FRIEND, TURTLE
> P.S. TO MAKE UP FOR SCARING YOU, I WILL
> TREAT EVERYBODY HERE TO AN EXQUISITE
> CHINESE CUISINE DINNER WHEN I WIN THE
> INHERITANCE.

"Poor Grace," Mr. Hoo said. "One daughter almost killed, the other one a bomber. Smart-aleck kid, first she blows up my kitchen, then she advertises my cuisine. Win the inheritance—ha! Maybe I'm lucky my son is a dumb jock."

"Boom," Madame Hoo said happily. She knew where they were going. Always on the day when Doug ate six eggs for breakfast, he ran around and around a big track and people clapped and gave him a shiny medal. Doug was so proud of his medals. She would never take them, not even the gold one, not even if it took her two more years to pay to go back to China. No, she would never take Doug's medals, and she would never sell that wonderful clock with the mouse who wears gloves and points to the time.

"You must be out of your mind, Jake Wexler. Go to a track meet with all those people pointing at me, snickering, saying: 'Look, there she is, the mother of Cain and Abel.' I'm not even sure I have the nerve to show my face at the Westing house tonight."

"Come on, Grace, it'll do you good." The podiatrist urged his reluctant wife down the third-floor hall. "Stop thinking about yourself for a change, think how poor Turtle must feel."

"Don't ever mention that child to me again, not after what she did to Angela. I never told you this, Jake, but I've always had a sinking sensation that the hospital mixed up the babies when Turtle was born."

"It's no wonder she wanted to blow us all up."

Grace's despair exploded in anger. "Oh, I get it, you're putting the blame on me. If you had given her a good talking to about kicking people when I asked, she might not have ended up a common criminal."

"Whatever became of that fun-loving woman I married, what was her name—Gracie Windkloppel?"

Grace quickly looked around to see if anyone had overheard that ugly name, but they were in the elevator, alone. "Oh, I know what people think," she complained. "Poor Jake Wexler, good guy, everybody's friend, married to that uppity would-be decorator. Well, Angela's not going to have to scrimp and save to make ends meet; she's going to marry a real doctor. I'll see to that."

"Sure you will, Grace, you'll see that Angela doesn't marry a loser like her father." A real doctor, she says. A podiatrist is a "real" doctor—well, it is these days, but when he went to school it was different. He could have gone back, taken more courses, but he was married by then, a father—oh, who's he kidding. Gracie's right, he is a loser. Next she'll mention having to give up her family because she married a Jew—no, she never brings that up, Grace with all her faults would never do that.

The elevator door opened to the lobby. Grace turned to her silent, sad-eyed husband, the loser. "Oh, Jake, what's happening to us? What's happening to me? Maybe they're right, maybe I'm not a nice person."

Jake pressed the CLOSE DOOR button and took his sobbing wife into his arms. "It's all right, Gracie, we're going home."

The doors opened on the second floor. "Mom! What's the matter with her, Daddy, she's crying? Gee, Mom, I'm sorry, it was just a few fireworks." If her mother ever found out who the real bomber was, she'd really go to pieces.

Turtle looked even more like a turtle today with her sad little face peering out of the kerchief tied under her small chin. "Let go of the door, Turtle," Jake said. "And have a good time at the track meet. You, too, Mrs. Baumbach."

Track meet? They weren't going to a track meet. And they sure were not going to have a good time.

Grace was still sobbing on Jake's shoulder as he led her into their apartment.

"Mother, what's the matter? What's wrong with her, Dad?"

"Nothing, Angela, your mother's just having a good cry. Why don't you and Ms. Pulaski leave us alone for a while."

"Come, Angela," Sydelle said, prodding her with the tip of one of her mismatched crutches. "We have some painting to do."

Angela looked back at the embracing couple; her father's face was buried in her weeping mother's tousled hair. They had not asked how she got home from the hospital (by taxi), they had not asked if she was still in pain (not much), they had not even peeked under the bandage to see if a scar was forming on her cheek (there was). Angela was on her own. Well, that's what she wanted, wasn't it? Yes, yes it was! She uttered a short laugh, and her hand flew up to the pain in her face.

"Do I look funny or something?"

"No, I wasn't laughing at you, Sydelle, I'd never laugh at you. It's just that suddenly everything seemed all right."

"It's all right, all right," her partner replied, unlocking the four locks on her apartment door. "Tonight's the night we're going to win it all."

Were they? The will said look for a name. They had a song, not a name.

"'O beautiful for spacious skies,'" Sydelle began to sing, "'For purple waves of grain.'"

"Not purple," Angela corrected her, "amber. 'For amber waves of grain.'"

Amber!

■ ■ ■ ■ ■ ■ ■ ■ ■ ■

Judge Ford paced the floor. Tonight Sam Westing would wreak his revenge unless she could prevent it. If she was right, the person in danger was the former Mrs. Westing. And if Turtle was right about the wax dummy, Sam Westing himself might be there to watch the fun.

There was a knock on her door. The judge was surprised to see Denton Deere, even more surprised when he wheeled Chris Theodorakis into her apartment. "Hello, Judge. Everybody else in the building is going to the track meet, it seems. I passed Sandy on the way out and he said you wouldn't mind having Chris for part of the afternoon. I've got to get back to the hospital."

"Hello, Judge F-Ford." Chris held out a steady hand which the judge shook.

"You're looking well, Chris."

"The m-medicine helped a lot."

"It's a big step forward," the intern said. Wrong word, the kid may never leave that wheelchair. "An even more effective medication is now in the developmental stage." That really sounded pompous. "Well, so long, Chris. See you tonight. Thanks, Judge."

"He knows lots of b-big words," Chris said.

"Yes, he certainly does," Judge Ford replied. What was she going to do with this boy here? She had so much to think about, so much to plan.

"You c-can work. I'll birdwatch," Chris offered, wheeling to the window, his binoculars banging against his thin chest.

"Good idea." The judge returned to her desk to study the newspaper clippings. Mrs. Westing: a tall, thin woman. She may no longer be thin, but she would still be tall. About sixty years old. If Sam Westing's former wife was one of the heirs, she had to be Crow.

"Look!" Chris shouted, startling the judge into dropping her files to the floor. She rushed to his side, thinking he needed help. "Look up there, Judge. Isn't it b-beautiful?"

High in the fall sky a V of geese was flying south. Yes, it was a beautiful sight. "Those are geese," the judge explained.

"C-canada goose (*Branta c-canadensis*)," Chris replied.

The judge was impressed, but she had work to do. Stooping to gather the dropped clippings, she was confronted by the face of Sam Westing. The photograph had been taken fifteen years ago. Those piercing eyes, the Vandyke beard, that short beaked nose (like a turtle's). The wax dummy in the coffin had been molded in the former image of Sam Westing as he had looked fifteen years ago—not as he looked now. She searched the folder. No recent photographs, no hospital records, no death certificate, just the accident report from the state highway police: Dr. Sidney Sikes suffered a crushed leg and Samuel W. Westing had severe facial injuries. Facial injuries! It was the face that had disappeared fifteen years ago, not the man. Westing had a different face, a face remodeled by plastic surgery. A different face and a different name.

Now what? Her gaze rested on her charge at the window. Feeling her eyes, Chris turned around. The boy has a nice smile.

■ ■ ■ ■ ■ ■ ■ ■ ■ ■ ■

"I hope you are better at filling cavities than making false teeth," Turtle said, gripping the arms of the dentist's chair. In a glass cabinet against the wall three rows of dentures grinned at her with crooked teeth, overlapping teeth, notched teeth.

"Those faults are what makes the dentures look real," the dentist explained. "Nothing in nature is quite perfect, you know. Now, open your mouth wide. Wider."

"Ow!" Turtle screamed before the probe touched tooth.

"Just relax, young lady, I'll tell you when to say 'Ow!'"

Turtle tried to think about other things. False teeth, buck-teeth—that rotten bucktoothed Barney Northrup stopped by this morning to tell the Wexlers they would have to pay for all the damage done by the bombs. Barney Northrup had called her parents "irresponsible" and had called her something worse, much worse. He sure was surprised by that kick; it was her hardest one ever.

"Now you can say 'Ow!'" The dentist unclipped the towel from her shoulder.

Turtle passed her tongue over the drilled tooth. She had not felt a thing, but the real pain was yet to come. Flora Baumbach was taking her to the beauty parlor to have her singed hair cut off.

■ ■ ■ ■ ■ ■ ■ ■ ■ ■ ■ ■

College teams from five states competed in the first indoor track meet of the season, but the big event, the mile run, was won by a high-school senior.

"That's my boy, that's my Doug," Mr. Hoo shouted, one voice among thousands cheering the youngster on his victory lap.

Cameras flashed as Doug posed, smiling broadly, index fingers high in the air. "I owe it all to my dad," he told reporters, and cameras flashed again as Doug flung an arm around the proud Mr. Hoo. Just wait until the next Olympics, the inventor thought. With Doug's feet and my innersoles, he'll run them all to the ground.

Later that evening Madame Hoo, chattering in unintelligible Chinese, made it known that she wanted Doug to wear his prize to the Westing house. Standing on tiptoe she placed the ribbon over his bent head and patted the shiny gold medal in place on his chest. "Good boy," she said in English.

■ ■ ■ ■ ■ ■ ■ ■ ■ ■ ■

A saddened Sandy returned to apartment 4D. "Hi, Chris. Did you talk to him, Judge?"

"Talk to whom?"

"Barney Northrup. He was waiting at the front door when I got back from the track meet, mad as a wet cat. Said he had lots of complaints about me—never being on duty, drinking on the job—lies like that. He fired me right on the spot. I told him you wanted to see him, figuring you might put in a good word so he'd let me stay on."

"No, Mr. McSouthers, I'm sorry, but I haven't seen Barney Northrup since I rented this apartment." Barney Northrup, was that Westing's disguise: false buckteeth, slick black wig, pasted-on moustache?

"Well, it's not the first time I got fired for no cause." The dejected doorman blew his nose loudly in a Westing Man-Sized Hankie. "Hey Chris, bet you don't know the Latin name of the red-headed woodpecker."

That was a hard one. Chris had to say *Melanerpes erythro-cephalus* very slowly.

"Some smart kid, hey, Judge? Chris, the judge and I have a little business to discuss. Excuse us for a minute."

Judge Ford joined the doorman in the kitchen. "Our game plan is this, Mr. McSouthers. We give no answer. No answer at all. Our duty is to protect Westing's ex-wife."

"Crow?" Sandy guessed.

"That's right."

"There's something else that's been bothering me, Judge. I know it sounds crazy, but, well, I found out Otis Amber doesn't live in the grocer's basement, and he's not as dumb as he pretends. He's a snoop and a troublemaker and I don't think he is who he says he is."

"And who do you think Otis Amber is?" the judge asked.

"Sam Westing!"

Judge Ford leaned against the sink and pressed her head against the cabinet. If Sandy was correct, she had played right into the man's hands—Sam Westing's hands.

■ ■ ■ ■ ■ ■ ■ ■ ■ ■ ■

"C'mon, Crow, you always like to get there early to open the door for people."

Crow had stopped in the middle of the steep road to stare up at the Westing house. "I've got a funny feeling that something evil is waiting for me up there, Otis. It's a bad house, full of misery and sin. He's still there, you know."

"Sam Westing is dead and buried. Come on, if we don't go we gotta give the money back, and we already spent it on the soup kitchen."

"I feel his presence, Otis. He's looking for a murderer, Violet's murderer."

"Stop scaring yourself with crazy notions, you sound like you're on the bottle again."

Crow strode ahead.

"I didn't mean that, Crow, honest. Look up there at that moon. Isn't it romantic?"

"Somebody's in real danger, Otis, and I think it's me."

23

LAWYER PLUM WAS there and one pair of heirs when Otis Amber danced into the game room. "He-he-he, the Turtle's lost its tail, I see."

Turtle slumped low in her chair. Flora Baumbach thought the short, sleek haircut was adorable, especially the way it swept forward over her little chin, but Turtle did not want to look adorable. She wanted to look mean.

The dressmaker fumbled past the wad of money in her handbag. "Here, Alice, I thought you might like to see this."

Turtle glanced at the old snapshot. It's Baba, all right, except younger. Same dumb smile. Suddenly she sat upright.

"That's my daughter, Rosalie," Flora Baumbach said. "She must have been nine or ten when that picture was taken."

Rosalie was squat and square and squinty, her protruding tongue was too large for her mouth, her head lolled to one side. "I think I would have liked her, Baba," Turtle said. "Rosalie looks like she was a very happy person. She must have been nice to have around."

Thump-thump, thump-thump. "Here come the victims," Sydelle Pulaski announced.

Angela greeted her sister with a wave of her crimson-streaked, healing hand. Turtle had convinced her not to confess: It would mean a criminal record, it would kill their mother, and no one would believe her anyhow. "I like your haircut."

"Thanks," Turtle replied. Now Angela had to love her forever.

Most of the heirs had to comment on Turtle's hair. "You look like a real businesswoman," Sandy said. "Well, that's an improvement," Denton Deere said. "You look n-nice," Chris said. Only Theo, bent over the chessboard, said nothing. White had moved the king's bishop since the last meeting. It was his move.

At last the stares turned from Turtle's hair to a more surprising sight. Judge Ford strode in as regally as an African princess, her noble head swathed in a turban, her tall body draped in yards of handprinted cloth. She slipped a note to Denton Deere then sailed to her place at table four. Goggle-eyed Otis Amber was speechless; they all were, except for Sandy. "Gee, that's a nifty outfit, Judge. Is that what you call ethnic?"

The judge did not reply.

Applaud, the local hero has arrived! Doug raised his arms, pointing his index fingers to the flaking gilt ceiling in the I'm-number-one sign, and acknowledged the clapping with a victory lap around the room.

"Here come the Wexlers," Mr. Hoo remarked, seating his puzzled wife at table one.

Turtle exchanged an anxious glance with Angela. The last time they saw their mother she was crying her head off; now the tears were gone from her bleary eyes, but she was staggering, giggling, her hair was a mess.

"Sorry we're late," Jake apologized. "We lost track of time." They had been clinking wineglasses in a small cafe (the cafe they used to go to before they were married), toasting good times. They had had many good times together, many good memories shared, it seems—three big wine bottles full.

Happy Grace waved at the heirs. She felt so wonderful, so overflowing with love for Jake, for everybody.

"Hi, Mom," Turtle called.

Grace blinked at a young short-haired girl. "Who's that?"

Jake greeted his partner with a "How are you this fine day?"

"Doug win," replied Madame Hoo.

Having opened the door to the last of the heirs, a tense and troubled Crow took her seat next to Otis Amber. Ghost-threatened, she waited for the unseen.

"Hey, lawyer, can we open these?" Otis Amber shouted, waving an envelope. A similar envelope lay on each table.

His forehead creased with uncertainty, Ed Plum fumbled through his papers. "I guess so" was his opinion.

Cheers erupted as the heirs withdrew the checks.

Again Judge Ford signed her name to the ten-thousand-dollar check and handed it to the doorman. "Here you are, Mr. McSouthers, this should tide you over until you find another job."

Sandy's heartfelt thanks were muffled by Sydelle Pulaski's loud "Shhhh!"

"Shhhhhhhh!" Grace Wexler mimicked, then she dropped her head into her crossed arms on the table and fell asleep to the sound of the lawyer's throat-clearing coughs.

> TWELFTH • *Welcome again to the Westing house. By now you have received a second check for ten thousand dollars. Before the day is done you may have won more, much more.*
>
> *Table by table, each pair will be called to give one, and only one, answer. The lawyer will record your response in case of a dispute. He does not know the answer. It is up to you.*

1 • MADAME SUN LIN HOO, *cook*
  JAKE WEXLER, *bookie*

Bookie? He really must have been distracted when he signed that receipt. Jake studied the five clues on the table:

OF   AMERICA   AND   GOD   ABOVE

Even knowing his wife's clues didn't help; he'd have to gamble on a long shot. "Say something," he said to his partner.

"Boom!" said Madame Hoo.

Ed Plum wrote *Table One: Boom.*

2 • FLORA BAUMBACH, *dressmaker*
  TURTLE WEXLER, *financier*

Turtle read a prepared statement: "In spite of the fact that the stock market dropped thirty points since we received our ten thousand dollars, we have increased our capital to $11,587.50, an appreciation of twenty-seven point eight percent calculated on an annual basis."

Flora Baumbach slapped a wad of bills on the table and two clinking quarters. "In cash," she said.

Ed Plum asked them to repeat their answer.

"Table two's answer is $11,587.50."

Sandy applauded. Turtle took a bow.

3 • CHRISTOS THEODORAKIS, *ornithologist*
    D. DENTON DEERE, *intern*

Ornithologist? His brother must have given him that fancy title when he filled in the receipt. Maybe he would become an ornithologist someday. He was a lucky person, getting that medicine and all. He didn't want to accuse anybody, not Judge Ford (apartment 4D), not Otis (grain) Amber, not the limper (just about everybody limped at one time or other—today Sandy was limping). "I think Mr. Westing is a g-good man," Chris said aloud. "I think his last wish was to do g-good deeds. He g-gave me a p-partner who helped me. He g-gave everybody the p-perfect p-partner to m-make friends."

"What is table three's answer?" the lawyer asked.

Denton Deere replied. "Our answer is: Mr. Westing was a good man."

4 • J. J. FORD, *judge*
    ALEXANDER MCSOUTHERS, *fired*

"We don't have an answer," the ex-doorman responded as planned.

The judge looked at table three. Denton Deere, her note in his hand, shook his head, which meant: No, Otis Amber has not had plastic surgery done on his face. The judge turned to table six. Otis Amber could not be Sam Westing (she was right to have trusted him). But Crow is expecting something to happen. Crow knows she is the answer, she knows she is the one.

5 ● GRACE WINDKLOPPEL WEXLER, *restaurateur*
   JAMES HOO, *inventor*

Grace raised her head. "Did someone say Windkloppel?"

"Never mind Windkloppel, it's our turn," Hoo snarled. The lawyer got names and positions all fouled up, and I've got a drunk for a partner. He prodded Grace to her feet.

Faces were swirling, the floor was swaying. Grace grabbed the edge of the floating table and gave her answer in a thick, slurred voice. "The newly decorated restaurant, Hoo's On First, the eatery of athletes, will hold its grand reopening on Sunday. Specialty of the day: fruited sea bass on purple waves."

Grace sat down where the chair wasn't. Turtle gasped, Angela looked away, the heirs tittered as Jake helped his wife up from the floor.

"What is table five's answer, please?" the lawyer pressed.

"Ed Plum," said Mr. Hoo.

"Yes, sir?"

"That's our answer: Ed Plum."

"Oh."

6 ● BERTHE ERICA CROW, *mother*
   OTIS AMBER, *deliverer*

"Mother? Did I write *mother*?" Crow mumbled.

"Is that your answer?" Ed Plum asked.

"I don't know," Otis Amber replied. "Is 'mother' our answer,

Crow?" He could have sworn she had again signed the receipt *Good Salvation Soup Kitchen*.

Crow repeated "mother," and that's what the lawyer wrote down.

7 • DOUG HOO, *champ*
  THEO THEODORAKIS, *writer*

Their clues: a chemical formula for an explosive and the letters *o-t-i-s*. Doug, basking in glory, didn't care. Theo stood, turned to the man he was about to accuse, and saw the scene in the soup kitchen, saw Otis Amber cooking soup for the dirty, hungry men. "No answer," Theo said sitting down.

8 • SYDELLE PULASKI, *victim*
  ANGELA WEXLER, *person*

Sydelle was dressed for the occasion in red and white stripes. Leaning on crutches decorated with white stars on a field of blue to match the cast on her ankle, she hummed into a pitch pipe and began to sing one note above the pitch she played.

> O beautiful for spacious skies,
> For amber waves of grain,
> For purple mountain majesties
> Above the fruited plain.

What a spectacle she made, her wide rear end sticking out, singing in that tuneless, nasal voice. The derisive smiles soon faded as, pair by pair, the heirs heard their code words sung.

> America! America!
> God shed His grace on thee,
> And crown thy good with brotherhood
> From sea to shining sea.

"Such a beautiful song," Grace Wexler slurred, but the others sat in somber silence. Even Turtle thought table eight had won.

"What is your answer?" Ed Plum asked.

"Our answer," Sydelle Pulaski announced with certainty, "is Otis Amber."

The heirs listened to the lawyer read the next document, but their eyes stayed fixed on table eight's answer: Otis Amber.

> **THIRTEENTH** ● *Okay, folks, there will be a short break before the big winner is announced. Berthe Erica Crow, please rise and go to the kitchen for the refreshments.*

Dazed with fear, Crow rose. The thirteenth section. Thirteen was an unlucky number.

Judge Ford told Sandy to follow her. "Hey, Crow, old pal, do me a favor and fill this for me," he said, handing her his flask as they left through the door. "I'll go on the wagon starting tomorrow. Promise."

Angela left the room, too, concerned over Crow's trance-like state. Turtle followed Angela to make sure she didn't end up in the fireworks room again. The judge remained seated, watching the remaining heirs, who were watching Otis Amber. The delivery boy had had enough of their suspicions; he swept a pointed finger across their range, imitating the sound of a machine gun: "Rat-a-tat-tat-tat-tat."

Crow and Angela came back with two large trays; Turtle returned empty-handed, puzzled but much relieved.

The judge joined Denton Deere and Chris at table three, bringing a plate of small cakes with her. "None of the heirs have had plastic surgery as far as I can tell," the intern remarked. "But your partner sure could have used some."

The judge studied Sandy McSouthers' prizefighter's face as he leaned against the open doorway. Their eyes met and he lifted his flask in salute. "Anybody want a drink?"

"Sure," Grace Wexler replied with a giggle, but Jake gave her a cup of strong black coffee instead.

"We must keep our wits about us, Mr. McSouthers," Judge Ford said, walking toward him. "Sam Westing has not made his final move."

"Nothing like Scotch to clear the head," he replied. He took a long swig, coughed, wiped his mouth on the sleeve of his uniform, and glared at Crow with narrowed, watery eyes.

Theo grinned down at the chess table. White had made another move, a careless move. He licked the cake crumbs from his fingers, wiped his hand on a Westing Paper Tea Napkin, and took his opponent's queen from the board. At least he had won the chess game.

Perched on a corner of table eight, the young lawyer tried to start a conversation with Angela, ignoring Sydelle Pulaski, who twice asked, "Surely *you* must have the answer, Mr. Plum?" She nudged her partner.

"Surely you must have the answer, Mr. Plum," Angela repeated sweetly.

"Oh, of course; at least, I assume I do," he replied. "My instructions are to open the documents one by one at the scheduled time." He checked his watch. "Oops!" He was one minute late.

Ed Plum hurried to the billiard table, tore open the next envelope, and pulled out the document, cutting his finger on the paper's edge.

FOURTEENTH • *Go directly to the library. Do not pass Go.*

■ WRONG ALL WRONG ■

24

GRACE WEXLER CLUNG unsteadily to Mr. Hoo's arm. "Where are we going?"

"Who knows," Hoo replied. "We didn't even pass Go."

Partner sat with partner at the long library table, moaning

with impatience as Ed Plum opened another envelope, removed a tagged key, tried to unlock the top right-hand desk drawer, reread the tag, unlocked the upper left-hand drawer, and found the next document:

FIFTEENTH • *Wrong! All answers are wrong!*

"What!" Sydelle Pulaski cried.

> *I repeat: Wrong! All answers are wrong! Partnerships are canceled; you are on your own. Alone.*
> *The lawyer will leave and return with the authorities at the appointed time. And time is running out. Hurry, find the name before the one who took my life takes another.*
> *Remember: It is not what you have, it's what you don't have that counts.*

Madame Hoo knew from the shifting eyes that a bad person was in the room. She was the bad person. They would find out soon. The crutch lady had her writing-book back, but all those pretty things she was going to sell, they wanted them back, too. She would be punished. Soon.

"How much time do we have?" Turtle asked.

Ed Plum left the library without answering. And locked the door!

"Oh my!" Flora Baumbach ran to the French doors. They opened.

Sydelle Pulaski complained of a chill, and the dressmaker had to shut the doors, but she left them unlatched, just in case.

Mr. Hoo said the tea tasted funny, maybe they had all been poisoned. Denton Deere diagnosed paranoia.

The doorman, who was pacing the room, replied that anyone who was not paranoid, after being told that the murderer would kill again, was really crazy. He stopped to pat Turtle's slumped shoulders. "Cheer up, my friend, the game's not over yet," Sandy whispered. "You still can win. I hope you do."

Otis Amber told everyone to sit where he could watch them.

Theo rose. "I think it's about time we played as a team and shared our clues and shared the inheritance."

With the murderer? Well, all right. Agreed.

Sydelle Pulaski still thought the answer had something to do with "America, the Beautiful." "Does anybody have a clue word that is not in the song?"

"I'm not sure," Doug said mischievously. "Sing it again."

No one cared for that idea. "*It is not what you have, it's what you don't have that counts,*" Jake Wexler reminded them. "Maybe some words in the song are missing from the clues."

That makes sense. "Does anyone have the word *amber*?" Mr. Hoo asked.

"Not again," Otis Amber groaned. "You heard the will, it said all answers were wrong. Well, I was one of the wrong answers."

"But Mr. Westing wrote the will before the game began." Sydelle argued. "Perhaps he assumed we weren't smart enough to find you out so soon."

Judge Ford did not interfere (Otis Amber could take care of himself). She had to be prepared to defend Crow when the time came.

Crow sat with her head bowed, waiting.

No one had the word *amber*, but two pairs had *am* in their clues. "Two *ams* do not an *amber* make," Sydelle declared. "Two *ams* stand for *America, America*."

"I've got *America*," Jake Wexler shouted. "I've got *America*."

Ravings of a madman, Mr. Hoo thought. The podiatrist, could he be the one?

Jake explained in a calmer voice. "The two *ams* could not stand for *America, America,* because one of my clues is *America*."

Sandy stood, took a long swig from his flask, coughed, then spoke in a hoarse voice. "We're getting nowhere. Why doesn't everybody hand in their clues so Ms. Pulaski can arrange them in order and we can see what's missing?"

Her eyes narrowed with suspicion, the judge watched Sandy collect the clues. "Just write them out again," he said to Turtle, who had eaten the originals. Then he placed the paper squares before the secretary and resumed his seat. What was her partner doing? Why was he playing into Westing's hands? He knows the answer, he knows he's leading the heirs to Crow. Again the judge studied the doorman's battered face: the scars; the bashed-in nose; the hard, blue eyes under those taped spectacles. The baggy uniform. Everyone was given the perfect partner, Chris said. Chris was right. She was paired with the one person who could confound her plans, manipulate her moves, keep her from the truth. Her partner, Sandy McSouthers, was the only heir she had not investigated. Her partner, Sandy McSouthers, was Sam Westing.

■ ■ ■ ■ ■ ■ ■ ■ ■ ■ ■

The secretary quickly arranged the clues in order:

O BEAUTIFUL FOR SPACIOUS SKIES
FOR AM WAVES OF GRAIN
FOR PURPLE MOUNTAIN MAJESTIES
ABOVE FRUITED PLAIN
AMERICA AM
GOD SHED HIS GRACE ON THEE
AND N THY GOOD WITH BROTHERHOOD
FROM SEA TO SHINING SEA

"The missing words," Sydelle Pulaski announced, "are *ber, the, erica,* and *crow.* Berthe Erica Crow!"

Crow paled.

Judge Ford stood. "May I have everyone's attention? Thank you. Please listen very carefully to what I have to say.

"We found the answer to Sam Westing's puzzle, now what are we going to do? Remember: We have no evidence of any kind against this unfortunate woman. We don't even have proof that Sam Westing was murdered.

"Can we accuse an innocent woman of a murder that has never been proved? Crow is our neighbor and our helper. Can we condemn her to a life imprisonment just to satisfy our own greed? For money promised in an improbable and illegal will? If so, we are guilty of a far greater crime than the accused. Berthe Erica Crow's only crime is that her name appears in a song. Our crime would be selling—yes, I said selling, selling for profit—the life of an innocent, helpless human being."

The judge paused to let her words sink in, then she turned to her partner. Her voice hardened. "As for the master of this vicious game . . ." She paused. What's happening to him?

"Uh—uh——UHHH!" Sandy's hand flew to his throat. He struggled to his feet, red-faced and gasping, and crashed to the floor in eye-bulging agony.

Jake Wexler and Denton Deere hurried to his aid. Theo pounded on the door, shouting for help. Ed Plum unlocked the door and two strange men rushed past him. One, carrying a doctor's bag, quickly limped on crooked legs to the side of the writhing doorman. "I'm Doctor Sikes. Everyone, please move away."

The heirs heard a low groan, then a rasping rattle . . . then nothing.

"Sandy! Sandy!" Turtle screamed, pushing through the restraining hands. She looked down on the doorman sprawled at her feet. His face was twisted in rigid pain; his mouth gaped over the chipped front tooth. The taped glasses had fallen from his blue eyes that were locked in an unseeing stare. Suddenly his body straightened in one last violent twitch. His right eye closed, then opened again, and Sandy moved no more.

"He's dead," Doctor Sikes said, gently turning her away.

"Dead?" Judge Ford repeated numbly. How could she have been so wrong? So very wrong?

A sob tore through Turtle's soul as she ran to Baba's comforting arms. "Baba, Baba, I don't want to play anymore."

■ ■ ■ ■ ■ ■ ■ ■ ■ ■ ■ ■

The second stranger, the sheriff of Westing county, herded them back to the game room. Without thinking, the heirs seated themselves at the assigned tables.

Turtle sat quietly; it was Flora Baumbach's turn to weep. Crow waited. Only the throbbing veins in her tightly clasped hands told of her torment.

"Excuse me, sir," Ed Plum said. "I realize this may seem inappropriate, but according to Samuel W. Westing's will, I must read another document on the hour."

The sheriff checked his watch. What kind of a madhouse is this? And there's something mighty fishy about this cocky kid-lawyer calling in the middle of dinner, insisting that I hurry right over. That was half an hour before anybody died. "Go ahead," he grumbled.

Plum cleared his throat three times under the sheriff's suspicious glare.

> SIXTEENTH • *I, Samuel W. Westing of Westingtown, born Sam "Windy" Windkloppel of Watertown (I had to change my name for business purposes. After all, who would buy a product called Windkloppel's Toilet Tissues? Would you?) do hereby declare that if no one wins, this will is null and void.*
>
> *So hurry, hurry, hurry, step right up and collect your prize. The lawyer will count off five minutes. Good luck and a happy Fourth of July.*

"Windkloppel, did someone say Windkloppel?" Grace Wexler slurred.

"I knew Westing wasn't an immigrant's name," Sydelle Pulaski said. "I knew it."

"The man was insane," Denton Deere diagnosed.

Shhh! They were struggling with their conscience. Millions and millions of dollars just for naming her name.

One minute is up!

The heirs stared at the answer: Berthe Erica Crow. A religious fanatic, maybe even crazy, but a murderer? They had no evidence that Westing was murdered, the judge said so.

Crow waited. She had not suffered enough for her sins, her penance was yet to begin.

Two minutes are up!

Two hundred million dollars, Turtle thought, but who gets it? The last part the lawyer read wasn't very businesslike. Besides, she could never peach on anybody, not even Crow. Who cares about anything anyhow—Sandy is dead, Sandy was her friend, now she'll never see him again—ever.

Judge Ford tried not to look at the empty chair at her table, McSouthers' chair. Her one concern was the safety of Crow. The judge watched the heirs and waited. Crow waited.

Three minutes are up!

Westing wasn't murdered, the judge said so, but what about Sandy? He was drinking from the flask Crow filled and he died choking. Poison?

Crow felt the eyes on her. The hating eyes. They scoffed at her beliefs, they joked about her soup kitchen. Only two people here mattered to her. She was so tired, so tired of waiting. Of waiting.

Four minutes are up!

"The answer is Berthe Erica Crow."

"No," Angela cried. "No, no!"

"She's crazy," Otis Amber shouted. "She don't know what she's saying."

"Yes I do, Otis," Crow said flatly and repeated her statement: "The answer is Berthe Erica Crow." She rose and turned to the confused lawyer. "I am Berthe Erica Crow. I am the answer and I am the winner. I give half of my inheritance to Otis Amber, to be used for the Good Salvation Soup Kitchen. I give the rest of the money to Angela."

■ WESTING'S WAKE ■

25

SANDY WAS DEAD. Crow had been arrested. The fourteen remaining heirs of Samuel W. Westing sat in Judge Ford's living room wondering what had happened.

"At least the guilt is not on our hands," Mr. Hoo said, trying to convince himself that a clear conscience was worth two hundred million dollars.

"Crow's going to jail," Otis Amber wailed, "and all you do is pat yourself on the back for not being a stoolie."

"Let me remind you that Crow confessed," Sydelle Pulaski reminded him.

"Crow only confessed to being the answer, nothing more," Angela said, pressing her hand against the tearing pain in her cheek.

"Even if Sam Westing wasn't murdered, like the judge said," Doug Hoo argued, "there was nothing wrong with Sandy until he drank from the flask Crow filled."

"If Crow is innocent," Theo said, "that means the murderer is still here in this room."

Flora Baumbach tightened her grip on Turtle, who was nestled in her arms.

"Poor Crow," Otis Amber muttered, "poor Crow."

"Poor Sandy, you should say," Turtle responded angrily. "Sandy's the one who's dead. Sandy was my friend."

"You should have remembered that before you kicked him," Denton Deere remarked.

"I never kicked Sandy, never."

The intern turned sideways in his chair in case of attack, but the kicker stayed slumped in sadness. "Well, someone kicked him today. That was one mean bruise he had on his shin."

"That's a lie, that's a disgusting lie," Turtle shouted. "The only person I kicked today was Barney Northrup and he deserved it. I didn't even see Sandy until tonight at the Westing house. Right, Baba?"

"That's right," Flora Baumbach said, handing Turtle a Westing Facial Tissue.

But Turtle was not about to cry again in front of everybody, like a baby. If only she could forget how he looked, suffering, dying: the twisted body, the chipped tooth, that horrible twitch, that one eye (that was the worst) that one eye blinking. Sandy used to wink at her like that when he was alive. When he was alive. Turtle blew her nose loudly to keep from sobbing.

"Sandy was my friend, too," Theo said. "I was playing chess with him in the game room, but he didn't know I knew."

"Why is everybody lying?" Turtle slumped further into Flora Baumbach's arm. Sandy was her friend, not Theo's. And Sandy didn't know how to play chess.

The judge, too, was surprised. "How can you be certain it was Mr. McSouthers you were playing with, Theo?"

"That's what partners are for. Doug watched the chess table to see who was moving the white pieces," Theo replied.

Again the track star thrust his I'm-number-one fingers high in the air.

Dumb jock, thought Mr. Hoo. Doesn't he realize this is a wake? But he is the champ. My son's the champ.

"Doug win," said Madame Hoo. They did not suspect her anymore. Good, very good. But it was so sad about the door guard.

Theo went on in a mournful voice. "I'm sort of glad Sandy didn't go back to the chessboard after my last move. He never knew he lost the game."

"Did you checkmate him?" the judge asked. Could she have been right about McSouthers after all? No. A disguise was one thing, but Sam Westing lose a game of chess? Never.

"Well, not exactly checkmate," Theo replied, "but Sandy would have had to resign. I took his queen."

The queen's sacrifice! The famous Westing trap. Judge Ford was certain now, but there were still too many unanswered questions. "I'm afraid greed got the best of you, Theo. By taking white's queen you were tricked into opening your defense. I know, I've lost a few games that way myself."

Theo recalled the position of the chessmen, thankful that his skin was too dark to reveal his blushing.

Turtle almost smiled. That Theo thinks he's so smart; well, Sandy showed him, Sandy beat him at chess. But Sandy didn't play chess. And she never kicked him either. Bucktoothed Barney Northrup was the one she kicked, not Sandy. But Sandy had the sore shin. Bucktoothed, chip-toothed, the crooked false teeth in the dentist's office (Sandy's dentist). "Cheer up, my friend, the game's not over. You still can win. I hope you do." Those were the last words Sandy said to her. He winked when he said that. Winked! One eye winked! Dead Sandy had winked at her!

Sandy had winked!

"Oh my," Flora Baumbach exclaimed as Turtle suddenly bolted from her arms.

"Angela, could I see your copy of the will?"

Angela handed it over (she could not refuse her sister anything, now).

■ ■ ■ ■ ■ ■ ■ ■ ■ ■ ■ ■

Turtle leaned against the dark window, poring over Sydelle Pulaski's transcript of the will:

FIRST. I returned to live among my
friends and my enemies. I came home to

> seek my heir, aware that in doing so I
> faced death. And so I did.

"To seek my heir," Turtle repeated to herself.

> Today I have gathered together my
> nearest and dearest, my sixteen nieces
> and nephews (Sit down, Grace Windsor
> Wexler!) to view the body of your Uncle
> Sam for the last time.
>   Tomorrow its ashes will be scattered
> to the four winds.

Winds? "Windkloppel," Turtle said aloud. Her mother had been right all along about being related to Sam Westing.

"Windkloppel," Grace mumbled. Jake patted her head.

"Windkloppel," the judge repeated. At least she could explain that. "Crow married a man named Windkloppel, who then changed his name to Westing. Berthe Erica Crow is the former wife of Samuel W. Westing. They had one child, a daughter, who drowned the night before her wedding. It was rumored that she killed herself rather than marry the man her mother had chosen for her. If Sam Westing blamed his wife for their daughter's death, then the sole purpose of this game was to punish Crow."

Crow was Sam Westing's ex-wife? The heirs found that hard to believe. "Then why would Mr. Westing give her a chance to inherit the estate?" Theo asked.

"M-maybe he wanted his enemies to for-g-give him," Chris said.

"Ha!" said Mr. Hoo, one of the enemies.

Turtle read on:

> SECOND. I, Samuel W. Westing, hereby swear
> that I did not die of natural causes. My life
> was taken from me—by one of you!

> The police are helpless. The culprit is far
> too cunning to be apprehended for this
> dastardly deed.

"What does dastardly mean?"

"Oh my!" Flora Baumbach was relieved to hear Jake Wexler define the word as "cowardly."

> I, alone, know the name. Now it is up to
> you. Cast out the sinner, let the guilty
> rise and confess.

> THIRD. Who among you is worthy to be
> the Westing heir? Help me. My soul shall
> roam restlessly until that one is found.

For the first time since Sandy died, Turtle smiled.

Judge Ford sat in glassy-eyed thought, elbows propped on the desk top, her chin resting on her folded hands. Why, indeed, was Crow an heir? Sam Westing could have pointed his clues at the Sunset Towers cleaning woman without naming her an heir.

"Crow's not going to inherit anything, not if she's in jail for murder," Otis Amber complained bitterly. "All your talk about chess and sacrificing queens. Crow's the one who's been sacrificed."

"What did you say?" the judge asked.

"I said Crow's the one who's been sacrificed."

Uttering a low groan, Judge Ford sank her head in her hands. The queen's sacrifice! She had fallen for it again. Westing had sacrificed his queen (Crow), distracting the players from the real game. Sam Westing was dead, but somehow or other he would make his last move. She knew it; she felt it deep in her bones. Sam Westing had won the game. "Stupid, stupid, stupid!"

The heirs stared in amazement. First they are told that Samuel W. Westing was married to their cleaning woman, now a judge is calling herself stupid. It couldn't be true.

"Sam Westing wasn't stupid," Denton Deere declared. "He was insane. The last part of the will was sheer lunacy. *Happy Fourth of July,* it said. This is November."

"It's November fifteenth," Otis Amber cried. "It's poor Crow's birthday."

Turtle looked up from the will. Crow's birthday? Sandy had bought a striped candle for his wife's birthday, a three-hour candle. The game is still on! Sam Westing came back to seek his heir. "You can still win. I hope you do," he said. How? How? *It is not what you have, it's what you don't have that counts.* Whatever it was she didn't have, she'd have to find it soon. Without letting the others know what she was looking for. "Judge Ford, I'd like to call my first witness."

■ **TURTLE'S TRIAL** ■

26

HOO WAS FURIOUS. "Haven't we had enough game-playing," he complained. "And led by a confessed bomber, no less."

Judge Ford rapped for silence with the walnut gavel presented to her by associates on her appointment to a higher court. Higher court? This was the lowest court she had ever presided at: a thirteen-year-old lawyer, a court stenographer who records in Polish, and the judge in African robes. Oh well, she had played Sam Westing's game, now she would play Turtle's game. The similarity was astounding; Turtle not only looked like her Uncle Sam, she acted like him.

"Ladies and gentlemen," Turtle began, "I stand before this court to prove that Samuel W. Westing is dead and that Sandy McSouthers is dead, but Crow didn't do it."

159

Pacing the floor, hands behind her back, she confronted each of the heirs in turn with a hard stare. The heirs stared back, not knowing if they were the jury or the accused.

Grace Wexler blinked up at her daughter. "Who's that?"

"The district attorney," Jake replied. "Go back to sleep."

Now frowning, now smiling a secret smile, Turtle acted the part of every brilliant lawyer she had seen on television who was about to win an impossible case. The only flaw in her imitation was an occasional rapid twist of her head. (She liked the grown-up feeling of shorter hair swishing around her face.)

"Let me begin at the beginning," she began. "On September first we moved into Sunset Towers. Two months later, on Halloween, smoke was seen rising from the chimney of the deserted Westing house." Her first witness would be the person most likely to have watched the house that day. "I call Chris Theodorakis to the stand."

Chris lay a calm hand on the Bible and swore to tell the truth, the whole truth, and nothing but the truth. What fun!

"You are a birdwatcher, Mr. Theodorakis, are you not?"

"Yes."

"Were you birdwatching on October thirty-first?"

"Yes."

"Did you see anyone enter the Westing house?"

"I s-saw s-somebody who limped."

Good, now she was getting somewhere. "Who was that limping person?"

"It was D-doctor Sikes."

"Thank you, you are excused." Turtle turned to her audience. "Doctor Sikes was Sam Westing's friend, a witness to the will, and his accomplice in this game. On the day in question he limped into the Westing house to build a fire in the fireplace. Why?" Her next witness might answer that.

■ ■ ■ ■ ■ ■ ■ ■ ■ ■ ■

Judge Ford instructed the witness to remove his aviator's helmet. His gray hair was tousled but barbered. "And place your gun in the custody of the court."

"Oh my!" Flora Baumbach gasped as Otis Amber unzipped his plastic jacket, pulled a revolver from his shoulder holster, and handed it to the judge, who locked the gun in her desk drawer.

Turtle was as startled as the other tenants. "Mr. Amber," she began bravely, "it seems that we are not all who we say we are. In other words, who exactly are you?"

"I am a licensed private investigator."

"Then why were you disguised as an idiot delivery boy?"

"It was my disguise."

Turtle was dealing with a practiced witness. "Mr. Amber, who employed you?"

"That's privileged information."

The judge interceded. "It would be best to cooperate, Mr. Amber. For Crow's sake."

"I had three clients: Samuel W. Westing, Barney Northrup, and Judge J. J. Ford."

Turtle stumbled over her next question. "What were you hired to do and when and what did you find out? Tell us everything you know." It was unsettling to see Otis Amber act like a normal human being.

"Twenty years ago, after his wife left him, Samuel W. Westing hired me to find Crow, keep her out of trouble, and make sure she never used the Westing name. I assumed this disguise for that purpose. I mailed in my reports and received a monthly check from the Westingtown bank until last week, when I was notified that my services were no longer needed. But Crow still needs me, and I'll stick by her, no matter what. I've grown fond of the woman; we've been together such a long time."

"How and why did Barney Northrup hire you?"

"Amber is second in the phone book under *Private Investigators;* maybe Joe Aaron's phone was busy that day. Anyhow, Barney Northrup wanted me to investigate six people."

"What six?"

"Judge J. J. Ford, George Theodorakis, James Hoo, Gracie Windkloppel, Flora Baumbach, and Sybil Pulaski. I made a mistake on the last one; I wasn't aware of the mix-up until I looked into Crow's early life for the judge. It seems I confused a Sybil Pulaski with a Sydelle Pulaski."

"Would you please repeat that," the court stenographer asked.

"Sydelle Pulaski," Otis Amber repeated, then turned to the judge. "I couldn't tell you about Crow's relationship to Sam Westing—conflict of interest, you understand."

Judge Ford understood very well. Sam Westing had predicted every move she would make. That's why Otis Amber, with his privileged information, was one of the heirs; that and to convince Crow (the queen) to play the game.

Turtle had more questions. "Are you saying that Barney Northrup didn't ask you to investigate Denton Deere or Crow or Sandy?"

"That's right. Denton Deere turned up in my report on Gracie Windkloppel—the Wexlers. Barney Northrup said he was looking to hire a cleaning woman for Sunset Towers, good pay and a small apartment, so I recommended Crow. I don't know how Sandy got the doorman's job."

"Mr. Amber, you were also hired by Judge Ford, I assume to find out who everybody really was. Did you investigate all sixteen heirs for the judge?"

"I didn't investigate the judge or her partner."

The judge bristled at the reminder of her stupidity.

"Therefore," Turtle continued, "you have never investigated the man we knew as Sandy McSouthers for any of your clients?"

"Never."

"One more question." It was the question she had planned to ask before learning that Otis Amber was not who he seemed to be. "On the afternoon of Halloween, when we were watching the smoke in the Westing house chimney, you told a story about a corpse on an Oriental rug."

"I saw it," Grace Wexler cried, "I saw him."

Turtle forgot the rules of the court and hurried to her mother. "Who did you see, Mom? Who? Who?"

(Terrified by the who's, Madame Hoo slipped away.)

"The doorman," Grace replied, lifting her dazed face to her husband. "He was dead. On an Oriental rug, Jake. It was awful."

Jake stroked his wife's hair. "I know, Gracie, I know."

Turtle returned to her witness. "Mr. Amber, did you tell that spooky story to dare one of us to go to the Westing house that night?"

"Not really. Sandy told me the story that morning, and we decided to scare you kids with it, being Halloween."

"Thank you, Mr. Amber, you may step down." (*Step down* was a term used in court; the floor was level here.) Turtle turned to her baffled audience. "A fire was started in the fireplace to call attention to the deserted house. Then a spooky story was told to dare someone to go into the house. That someone was me. I sneaked in the house, followed Dr. Sikes' whispers, and found the corpse of Samuel W. Westing in bed. I now call D. Denton Deere to the stand."

■ ■ ■ ■ ■ ■ ■ ■ ■ ■ ■ ■

Turtle stared at her most unfavorite heir. "Intern Deere, you saw the body of Samuel W. Westing in the coffin. Did he appear to have been poisoned?"

"I could not say; he was embalmed."

"You are under oath, Intern Deere. Do you swear that the body of Samuel W. Westing was embalmed?"

What kind of a trick question was that? "I cannot swear to it, no. I did not examine the body in the coffin."

"Could the body in the coffin, which you did not examine, have been no body at all? Could it have been a wax dummy dressed in the costume of Uncle Sam?"

"I am not an expert on wax dummies."

"Yes or no?"

"Yes, it's possible, anything is possible." What's the brat driving at? Or is she just trying to make a fool of me?

"Intern Deere, you may not be an expert in wax dummies, but you are an expert in medical diagnosis, and you did examine the body of Sandy McSouthers. Correct?"

"Yes to the first question, no to the second. I did not examine Sandy; I tried to make him comfortable until help arrived. He was still alive when Doctor Sikes took over."

Turtle turned quickly to conceal her smile. "But surely you saw enough symptoms to make one of your famous diagnosises." She peered at the judge from the corner of her eye. That last word didn't sound right.

"Coronary thrombosis," the intern diagnosed, "but that's just an educated guess. In simple language: heart attack."

"Then Sandy could not have died of an overdose of lemon juice, which is what I saw Crow put in his flask?" Turtle could have called on Angela to testify to that, but she didn't want her screwy sister confessing all over the place.

"I never heard of anyone dying as a result of lemon juice consumption," the expert replied.

"One more question, Intern Deere. Do you swear that Sandy had a bruise on his shin resulting from a kick?"

"Absolutely. I should know, having been the recipient of such a kick myself."

"You may step down."

■ ■ ■ ■ ■ ■ ■ ■ ■ ■ ■

"I call Sydelle Pulaski to the stand. SYDELLE PULASKI!"

Overcome with excitement, the secretary had to be helped to her feet for the oath-taking.

"Ms. Pulaski, I must compliment you on your good thinking in taking down the will in shorthand."

"Professional habit."

"This looks professional, all right. The typing is perfect—well, almost perfect. It seems you left out the last word in section three:

> The estate is at the crossroads. The heir
> who wins the windfall will be the one
> who finds the

"Finds the what, Ms. Pulaski? Finds the what?"

Sydelle squirmed under Turtle's hard stare. *Leave it to the brat to discover my one error.* "There was so much talking I couldn't hear the last word."

"Come now, Ms. Pulaski, you claim to be a professional."

Hounding the witness and doing it quite well, Judge Ford thought, coming to the secretary's defense. "I don't think anyone heard the word, Turtle. Mr. McSouthers made a joke about ashes at that point."

"You are excused, Ms. Pulaski," Turtle said offhandedly, her eyes on the will. The judge was right. Sandy had joked about ashes scattered to the winds. *Winds, Windy Windkloppel, no, it still didn't make sense. It is not what you have, it's what you don't have that counts*—maybe no word was ever there. She read on:

> FOURTH. Hail to thee, O land of
> opportunity! You have made me, the
> son of poor immigrants, rich, powerful,
> and respected.
> So take stock in America, my heirs,
> and sing in praise of this generous
> land. You, too, may strike it rich who
> dares play the Westing game.

FIFTH. Sit down, Your Honor, and read
the letter this brilliant young attorney
will now hand over to you.

"Judge Ford, could you introduce as evidence the letter that brilliant young attorney handed over to you?"

"It is just the usual certification of sanity, signed by Doctor
Sikes," the judge replied as she removed the envelope from her files.
But the letter was gone; the envelope now contained a receipt:

Check received, November 1	$ 5,000
Check received, November 15	+5,000
Total amount paid by Judge Ford	$10,000
Cost of educating Josie-Jo Ford	-10,000
Amount owed to Sam Westing	0

"I'm afraid the original letter has been replaced by a personal
message. It has no bearing on this case, and . . ."

"Yes, please." A trembling Madame Hoo stood before the judge.
"For to go to China," she said timidly, setting a scarf-tied bundle
on the desk. Weeping softly, the thief shuffled back to her seat.

The judge unknotted the scarf and let the flowered silk float
down around the booty: her father's railroad watch, a pearl
necklace, cuff links, a pin and earrings set, a clock. (Grace Wexler's silver cross never did turn up.)

"My pearls," Flora Baumbach exclaimed with delight.
"Wherever did you find them, Madame Hoo? I'm so grateful."

Madame Hoo did not understand why the round little lady
was smiling at her. Cautiously she peered through her fingers.
Oh! The other people did not smile. They know she is bad. And
Mr. Hoo, his anger is drowned in shame.

"Perhaps stealing is not considered stealing in China," Sydelle
Pulaski said in a clumsy gesture of kindness.

The judge rapped her gavel. "Let us continue with the case on hand. Are you ready, counselor?"

"Yes, Your Honor, in a minute." Turtle approached the frightened thief. "Here, you can keep it."

With shaking hands Madame Hoo took the Mickey Mouse clock from Turtle and clutched the priceless treasure to her bosom. "Thank you, good girl, thank you, thank you."

"That's okay."

The heirs were anxious for the trial to continue. They pitied the poor woman, but the scene was embarrassing.

■ ■ ■ ■ ■ ■ ■ ■ ■ ■ ■

One half hour to go. Turtle was so close to winning she could feel it, taste it, but still the answer eluded her. "Ladies and gentlemen, who was Sam Westing?" she began. "He was poor Windy Windkloppel, the son of immigrants. He was rich Sam Westing, the head of a huge paper company. He was a happy man who played games. He was a sad man whose daughter killed herself. He was a lonely man who moved to a faraway island. He was a sick man who returned home to see his friends and relatives before he died. And he did die, but not when we thought he did. Sam Westing was still alive when the will was read."

The judge rapped for order.

Turtle continued. "The obituary, probably phoned in to the newspaper by Westing himself, mentioned two interesting facts. One: Sam Westing was never seen after his car crashed. Two: Sam Westing acted in Fourth of July pageants, fooling everybody with his clever disguises. Therefore I submit that Sam Westing was not only alive, Sam Westing was disguised as one of his own heirs.

"No one would recognize him. With that face bashed in from the car crash, his disguise could be simple: a baggy uniform, a chipped front tooth, broken eyeglasses."

Sandy?

Does she mean Sandy?

The judge had to pound her gavel several times.

"Yes, ladies and gentlemen," Turtle went on, "Sam Westing was none other than our dear friend Sandy, the doorman. But Sam Westing did not drink, you say. Neither did Sandy. I used his flask on Halloween and there was a funny aftertaste in my pop, but not of whiskey; I know how whiskey tastes, because I use it for toothaches. It was medicine. Sandy was a sick man, and the flask was part of his disguise, but it also contained the medicine that kept him alive."

Turtle surveyed her stupefied audience. Good, they bought her little fib. "As I said earlier, I saw Crow fill the flask with lemon juice in the kitchen, but I saw something even more interesting on my way back to the game room: I saw Sandy coming out of the library. Sam Westing, as Sandy, wrote the last part of the will *after* the answers were given, then locked it in the library desk with a duplicate key.

"But what about the murder, you ask," Turtle said, even though no one had asked. "There was no murder. The word murder was first mentioned by Sandy, to put us off the track. *I did not die of natural causes,* the will says. *My life was taken from me—by one of you!* Sam Westing's life was taken from him when he became Sandy McSouthers. And Sandy died when his medicine ran out." Turtle paused in a pretense of letting the heirs mull over her last words, trying to figure out what to do next.

Why did Turtle leave out Barney Northrup, the judge wondered. She knows Northrup and McSouthers were the same man because of the bruised shin. Either she doesn't want to confound the jury, or she has no more idea than I have why Sam Westing had to play two roles.

Why did Sam Westing have to play *two* roles, Turtle wondered. He had a big enough part as the doorman without playing the real-estate man as well. Why *two* roles? No, not two, three. Windy Windkloppel took three names; one: Samuel W. Westing; two: Barney Northrup; three: Sandy McSouthers.

The judge had a question. "Surely Mr. McSouthers could have had his prescription refilled, or are you implying he committed suicide?"

"Pardon me?" Turtle was searching the will.

> The estate is at the crossroads. The heir
> who wins the windfall will be the one
> who finds the
>
> FOURTH.

That's it, that has to be it: *The heir who wins the windfall will be the one who finds the fourth!* Windy Windkloppel took four names, and she knew who the fourth one was! Keep calm, Turtle Alice Tabitha-Ruth Wexler. Slowly, very slowly, turn toward the judge, act dumb, and ask her to repeat the question. "I'm sorry, Your Honor, would you repeat the question?"

Turtle knows something. The judge had seen that expression before. Sam Westing used to look like that just before he won a game. "I asked if you consider Sandy's death a suicide."

"No, ma'am," Turtle said sadly. Very sadly. "Sandy McSouthers—Sam Westing suffered terribly from a fatal disease. He was a dying man who chose his time to die. Let me read from the will:

> SIXTH. Before you proceed to the game
> room there will be one minute of silent
> prayer for your good old Uncle Sam.

"Ladies and gentlemen, heirs (for we all inherited something), let us bow our heads in silent prayer for our benefactor Sam Westing, alias Sandy the doorman."

"Crow!" Otis Amber leaped to his feet as Ed Plum led the cleaning woman through the door.

27

HIS AVIATOR'S HELMET again flapping over his ears, Otis Amber danced up to his soup-kitchen companion, flung his arms around the taut body, and squeezed her tightly. "Hey Crow old pal, old pal, old pal."

"They said I was innocent, Otis. They said I was innocent," she replied vaguely.

Angela, too, wanted to hug her in welcome, but closeness was not possible for either of them. Instead, Angela offered a crooked smile. Crow nodded and lowered her eyes, only to raise them to Madame Hoo, clutching a Mickey Mouse clock. "Things very good," Madame Hoo said, extending her free hand and shaking Crow's hand up and down.

"It was all a regrettable mistake," Ed Plum explained to the judge. "Can you imagine, that sheriff wanted to arrest me, not Crow—me, Edgar Jennings Plum—he wanted to arrest the attorney! Fortunately, the coroner determined that Mr. McSouthers died of a heart attack, as did Samuel W. Westing."

"Then Turtle's right," Theo said. "There was no murder. The coroner was part of the plot."

Ed Plum had no idea what Theo was talking about. Masking his ignorance with arrogance, he continued. "I had my suspicions about this entire affair from the start. I came here for one reason only: to announce my resignation from all matters regarding the Westing estate, with sincere apologies to all concerned."

"Wasn't there a last document?" Judge Ford asked, knowing that Sam Westing had to make his last move.

"Yes, but as I no longer take a legal interest . . ."

"Please turn it over to the court."

Baffled by the word "court," the lawyer set the envelope on the desk and found his way out of Sunset Towers.

Without once clearing her throat, Judge Ford proceeded to read the final page of the will of Samuel W. Westing.

SEVENTEENTH • *Good-bye, my heirs. Thanks for the fun and games. I can rest in peace knowing I was loved as your jolly doorman.*

EIGHTEENTH • *I, Samuel W. Westing, otherwise known as Sandy McSouthers and others, do hereby give and bequeath all the property and possessions in my name as follows:*

To all of you, in equal shares, the deed to Sunset Towers;

And to my former wife, Berthe Erica Crow, the ten-thousand-dollar check forfeited by table one, and two ten-thousand-dollar checks endorsed by J. J. Ford and Alexander McSouthers.

NINETEENTH • *The sun has set on your Uncle Sam. Happy birthday, Crow. And to all of my heirs, a very happy Fourth of July.*

Judge Ford set the document down. "That's it."

That's it? What about the two hundred million dollars, the heirs wanted to know.

"We lost the game," the judge explained, staring at Turtle, her face a mask of sad, childlike innocence as she nestled once again in Flora Baumbach's arms. "I think."

Turtle rose and walked to the side window, seeking the Westing house, which stood invisible in the moon-clouded night. (Hurry up, Uncle Sam, I can't keep up this act much longer. The candle must have burned through the last stripe by now.)

Behind her the discontented heirs grumbled: He made fools of us all. He played us like puppets. He was a g-good m-man. He was a vengeful man, a hateful man. Windkloppel? He tricked us, the cheat. A madman, stark raving mad.

"Oh my, oh my, just listen to you," Flora Baumbach said. "You each have ten thousand dollars more than you started with and an apartment building to boot. The man is dead, so why not think the best?"

BOOM!

BOOM!

BOOM!

"Happy Fourth of July," Turtle shouted as the first rockets lit up the Westing house, lit up the sky.

BOOM-BOOM-BOOM-BOOM.

BOOM!!!

The heirs gathered around Turtle at the window.

BOOM! Stars of all colors bursting into the night, silver pin-wheels spinning, golden lances up-up-BOOM! crimson flashes flashing blasting, scarlet showers BOOM! emerald rain BOOM! BOOM! orange flames, red flames leaping from the windows, sparking the turrets, firing the trees. . . .

"BOOM!" cried Madame Hoo, clapping her hands with delight.

The great winter fireworks extravaganza, as it came to be called, lasted only fifteen minutes. Twenty minutes later the Westing house had burned to the ground.

"Happy birthday, Crow," Otis Amber said, reaching for her hand.

■ ■ ■ ■ ■ ■ ■ ■ ■ ■ ■

The orange glow of the morning sun had just begun its climb up the glass front of Sunset Towers when Turtle set out to collect the prize. She pedaled north past the cliff, still smoldering with the charred remains of the Westing house. Reaching the crossroads, she turned into the narrow lane whose twisting curves mimicked the shoreline.

The heir who wins the windfall will be the one who finds the fourth. It was so simple once you knew what you were looking for. Sam *West*ing, Barney *North*rup, Sandy Mc*South*ers (west, north, south). Now she was on her way to meet the fourth identity of Windy Windkloppel. She could probably have figured out the address, too, instead of looking it up in the Westingtown phone book—there it was, number four Sunrise Lane.

A long driveway, its privacy guarded by tall spruce, led to the modern mansion of the newly elected chairman of the board of Westing Paper Products Corporation. Turtle climbed the stairs, rang the bell, and waited. The door opened.

Turtle felt her first grip of panic as she confronted the crippled doctor. Could she have been wrong? "I'd like to see Mr. Eastman, please," she said nervously. "Tell him Turtle Wexler is here."

"Mr. Eastman is expecting you," Doctor Sikes said. "Go straight down the hall."

The hall had an inlaid marble floor (no Oriental rugs). Reaching its end, she entered a paneled library (this one filled with books). There he was, sitting at the desk.

Julian R. Eastman rose. He looked stern. And very proper. He wore a gray business suit with a vest, a striped tie. His shoes were shined. He limped as he walked toward her, not the crooked limp of Doctor Sikes, just a small limp, a painful limp. Again Turtle was gripped by panic. He seemed so different, so important. She shouldn't have kicked him (the Barney Northrup him). He was coming closer. His watery-blue eyes stared at her over his rimless half-glasses. Hard eyes. His teeth were white, not quite even (no one would ever guess they were false). He was smiling. He wasn't angry with her, he was smiling.

"Hi, Sandy," Turtle said. "I won!"

■ **AND THEN . . .** ■

28

TURTLE NEVER TOLD. She went to the library every Saturday afternoon, she explained (which was partly true). "Make your move, Turtle, you don't want to be late for the wedding."

The ceremony was held in Shin Hoo's restaurant. Grace Wexler, recovered from a world-record hangover, draped a white cloth over the liquor bottles and set a spray of roses on the bar. No drinks would be served today.

Radiant in her wedding gown of white heirloom lace, the bride walked down the aisle, past the tables of well-wishers, on the arm of Jake Wexler. Mr. Hoo, the best man, beamed with pride at her light footsteps as he supported the knee-knocking, nervous groom.

A fine red line of a scar marked Angela's check, but she looked content and lovely as ever in her pale blue bridesmaid's gown. The other bridesmaid wore pink and yellow with matching crutches.

The guests cried during the wedding and laughed during the reception. Flora Baumbach smiled and cried at the same time. "You did a good job altering the wedding dress, Baba," Turtle said, which made the dressmaker cry even harder.

"A toast to the bride and groom," Jake announced, raising his glass of ginger ale. "To Crow and Otis Amber!"

The heirs of Uncle Sam Westing clinked glasses with the members of the Good Salvation Soup Kitchen, sobered up for this happy occasion. "To Crow and Otis Amber!"

■ ■ ■ ■ ■ ■ ■ ■ ■ ■ ■ ■

Apartment 4D was bare. For the last time Judge Ford stared out the side window to the cliff where the Westing house once stood. She would never solve the Westing puzzle; perhaps it was just as well. Her debt would finally be repaid—with interest; the money she received from the sale of her share of Sunset Towers would pay for the education of another youngster, just as Sam Westing had paid for hers.

"Hi, Judge Ford, I c-came to say g-good-bye," Chris said, wheeling himself through the door.

"Oh hello, Chris, that was nice of you, but why aren't you studying? Where's your tutor?" She looked at the binoculars hanging from his neck. "You haven't been birdwatching again, have you? There will be plenty of time for birds later; first you must catch up on your studies if you want to get into a good school." Good heavens, she was beginning to sound like Mr. Hoo.

"Will you c-come to see m-me?" Chris asked. "It g-gets sort of lonely with Theo away at c-college."

The judge gave him one of her rare smiles. He was a bright youngster ("Real smart," Sandy had said), he had a good future (Sandy had said that, too), he needed her influence and the extra money, but she might smother him with her demands. "I'll see you when I can, and I'll write to you, Chris. I promise."

■ ■ ■ ■ ■ ■ ■ ■ ■ ■ ■

Hoo's Little Foot-Eze (patent pending) was selling well in drugstores and shoe repair shops.

"Once we capture the Milwaukee market I'll take you to China," James Hoo promised his business partner.

"Okay," Madame Hoo replied, toting up accounts on her abacus. No hurry. She had many friends in Sunset Towers now. And no more cooking, no more tight dresses slit up her thigh. Her husband had bought her a nice pantsuit to wear when they called on customers, and for her birthday Doug had given her one of his medals to wear around her neck.

■ ■ ■ ■ ■ ■ ■ ■ ■ ■ ■

The secretary to the president of Schultz Sausages was back on the job. Her ankle mended, Sydelle Pulaski had discarded her crutches. She had all the attention she could handle without them; after all, she was an heiress now. (It wasn't polite to ask how much, but everyone knew Sam Westing had millions.) Of course she could retire to Florida, she said, but what would poor

Mr. Schultz do without her? And then one unforgettable Friday Mr. Schultz, himself, took her to lunch.

■ ■ ■ ■ ■ ■ ■ ■ ■ ■ ■

Jake Wexler had given up his private practice (both private practices) now that he had been appointed consultant to the governor's inquiry panel for a state lottery (thanks to a recommendation by Judge Ford). Grace was proud of him, and his daughters were doing well. In fact everything was fine, just fine.

Hoo's On First was a great success. Grace Wexler, the new owner, offered free meals to the sports figures who came to town, and everyone wanted to eat where the athletes ate. The restaurant's one windowless wall was covered with autographed photographs of Brewers, Packers, and Bucks. Grace straightened the framed picture of a smiling champion, signed: *To Grace W. Wexler, who serves the number-one food in town—Doug Hoo*. She certainly was a lucky woman: a respected restaurateur, wife of a state official, and mother of the cleverest kid who ever lived. Turtle was going to be somebody someday.

A narrow scar remained, and would always remain, on Angela's cheek. It was slightly raised, and she had developed a habit of running her fingers along it as she pored over her books. Enrolled in college again, she lived at home to save money for the years of medical school ahead. She had returned the engagement ring to Denton Deere; she had not seen him since Crow's wedding. Ed Plum had stopped calling after ten refusals. Angela had neither the time nor the desire for a social life what with studying, her weekly shopping date with Sydelle, and Sundays spent helping Crow and Otis in the soup kitchen.

"Study, study, study," Turtle said.

Angela saw little of her sister, who was either at school, in Flora Baumbach's apartment, or at the library. "Hi, Turtle, how come you're so happy today?"

"The stock market jumped twenty-five points."

The newlyweds, Crow and Otis Amber, moved into the apartment above the Good Salvation Soup Kitchen. The storefront mission had been renovated and expanded with the money from the inheritance. Grace Wexler had supervised the decorations: copper pots hung from the ceiling; the pews were padded with flowered cushions and fitted with hymnbook pockets and drop-leaf trays. There was meat in the soup and fresh bread every day.

▓ FIVE YEARS PASS ▓

29

THE FORMER DELIVERY boy danced into the Hoos' new lakefront home. "Let's give a cheer, the Ambers are here!" Otis came to celebrate Doug's victory, wearing the old zippered jacket and aviator's helmet. He had even let a stubble grow on his chin. The only thing missing was his delivery bike (they had come in the soup-kitchen van).

"Thank you for the generous donation, Mr. Hoo. God bless you," Crow said. "Otis and I distributed the innersoles among our people. It helped their suffering greatly." She looked worn, her skin pulled tight against the fragile bones, and she still wore black.

Mr. Hoo, on the other hand, was stouter and less angry. In fact, he was almost happy. Business was booming. Milwaukee loved Hoo's Little Foot-Eze, and so did Chicago and New York and Los Angeles, but he still had not taken his wife to China.

Theo Theodorakis, graduate of journalism school, cub reporter, held up the newspaper, hot off the press:

OLYMPIC HERO COMES HOME

Four columns were devoted to the history and achievement of the gold medal winner who had set a new record for the 1500-

meter run. Theo had not actually written the article on the local hero, but he had sharpened pencils for the reporter who did.

"Take a bow, Doug," Mr. Hoo said, beaming.

Doug leaped on a table and thrust his index fingers high in the air. "I'm number one!" he shouted. The Olympic gold medal hung from his neck, confetti from the parade dotted his hair. The Westing heirs cheered.

■ ■ ■ ■ ■ ■ ■ ■ ■ ■ ■

"Hello, Jake, I'm so glad you could come," Sunny (as Madame Hoo was now called) said, shaking the hand of the chairman of the State Gambling Commission.

"Boom!" Jake Wexler replied.

■ ■ ■ ■ ■ ■ ■ ■ ■ ■ ■

"Hello, Angela." Denton Deere had grown a thick moustache. He was a neurologist. He had never married.

"Hello, Denton." Angela's golden hair was tied in a knot on the nape of her neck. She wore no makeup. She was completing her third year of medical school. "It's been a long time."

"Remember me?" Sydelle Pulaski wore a red and white polka-dot dress and leaned on a red and white polka-dot crutch. She had sprained her knee dancing a tango at the office party.

"How could I ever forget you, Ms. Pulaski?" Denton said.

"I'd like you to meet my fiancé, Conrad Schultz, president of Schultz Sausages."

"How do you do."

■ ■ ■ ■ ■ ■ ■ ■ ■ ■ ■

"Judge Ford, I'd like you to meet my friend, Shirley Staver." Chris Theodorakis was in his junior year at college. A medication, recently discovered, kept his limbs steady and his speech well controlled. He sat in a wheelchair, as he always would.

"Hello, Shirley," the judge said. "Chris has written so much about you. I'm sorry I'm such a poor correspondent, Chris; I found myself in a tangle of cases this past month." She was a judge on the United States Circuit Court of Appeals.

"Chris and I were both chosen to go on a birdwatching tour to Central America this summer," Shirley said.

"Yes, I know."

■ ■ ■ ■ ■ ■ ■ ■ ■ ■ ■

For old times' sake Grace Wexler catered the party herself and passed among the guests with a tray of appetizers. She owned a chain of five restaurants now: Hoo's On First, Hoo's On Second, Hoo's On Third, Hoo's On Fourth, Hoo's On Fifth.

"Who's that attractive young woman talking with Flora Baumbach?" Theo asked.

"Why, that's my daughter Turtle. She's really grown up, hasn't she? Second year of college and she's only eighteen. Calls herself T. R. Wexler now."

T. R. Wexler was radiant. Earlier that day she had won her first chess game from the master.

■ THE END? ■

30

TURTLE SPENT THE night at the bedside of eighty-five-year-old Julian R. Eastman. T. R. Wexler had a master's degree in business administration, an advanced degree in corporate law, and had served two years as legal counsel to the Westing Paper Products Corporation. She had made one million dollars in the stock market, lost it all, then made five million more.

"This is it, Turtle." His voice was weak.

"You can die before my very eyes, Sandy, and I wouldn't believe it."

"Show some respect. I can still change my will."

"No you can't. I'm your lawyer."

"That's the thanks I get for that expensive education. How's the judge?"

"Judge Ford has just been appointed to the United States Supreme Court."

"What do you know, honest Josie-Jo on the Supreme Court. She was a smart kid, too, but she never once beat me at chess. Tell me about the others, Turtle. How's poor, saintly Crow?"

"Crow and Otis are still slopping soup," Turtle fibbed. Crow and Otis Amber had died two years ago, within a week of each other.

"And that funny woman with the painted crutches, what's her name?"

"Sydelle Pulaski Schultz. She and her husband moved to Hawaii. Angela keeps in touch."

"Angela. And how is your pretty sister, the bomber?"

Turtle never knew he knew. "Angela is an orthopedic surgeon." Julian R. Eastman was an old man, but suddenly his mind, too, was old. For the first time since the Westing game he was wearing the dentures with the chipped front tooth. He had turned back to his happiest times. Sandy was dying, he was really dying. Turtle held back her tears. "Angela and Denton Deere are married. They have a daughter named Alice."

"Alice. Doesn't Flora Baumbach call you Alice?"

"She used to, she calls me T. R. as everyone does."

"How is the dressmaker, Turtle? Tell me about them, tell me about all of them."

Flora Baumbach had given up dressmaking when she moved in with Turtle years ago. "Baba is well, everyone is well. Mr. and Mrs. Theodorakis (remember, they had the coffee shop in Sunset

Towers), they retired to Florida. Chris and his wife Shirley teach ornithology at the university. They're both professors. Chris discovered a new subspecies on his last trip to South America; it's named after him: the something-Christos parrot."

"The something-Christos parrot, I like that. And the track star? Has he won any more medals?"

"Two Olympic golds in a row. Doug is a sports announcer on television."

"And how is Jimmy Hoo's invention going? I gave him the idea, you know."

"It looks like a real winner, Sandy." Mr. Hoo, too, was dead. Sunny Hoo finally made her trip to China, but returned to carry on the business.

"And tell me about my niece, Gracie Windkloppel. Does she still think she's a decorator?"

"Mom went into the restaurant business, has a chain of ten. Nine are quite successful. I keep telling her to give up on Hoo's On Tenth, to cut her losses, but she's stubborn as ever. I guess she hangs on to it because it's in Madison, to be near Dad. He's now the state crime commissioner."

"He's well qualified for the job. And your husband, how's his writing coming along?"

He had remembered. "Theo's doing fine. The first novel sold about six copies, but it got great reviews. He's just about finished with his second book."

"And when are you two going to have children?"

"Some day." Turtle and Theo had decided against having children because of the possibility of inheriting Chris's disease. "If it's a boy we'll name him Sandy, and if it's a girl, well, I guess we can name her Sandy, too."

The old man's voice was barely audible now. "Did you say Angela had a little girl?"

"Yes, Alice, she's ten years old."

"Is she pretty like her mother?"

"I'm afraid not, she looks a lot like you and me."

"Turtle?"

"Yes, Sandy."

"Turtle?"

"I'm right here, Sandy." She took his hand.

"Turtle, tell Crow to pray for me."

His hand turned cold, not smooth, not waxy, just very, very cold.

Turtle turned to the window. The sun was rising out of Lake Michigan. It was tomorrow. It was the Fourth of July.

■ ■ ■ ■ ■ ■ ■ ■ ■ ■ ■

Julian R. Eastman was dead; and with him died Windy Windkloppel, Samuel W. Westing, Barney Northrup, and Sandy McSouthers. And with him died a little of Turtle.

No one, not even Theo, knew her secret. T. R. Wexler was understandably sad over the death of the chairman of the board of the Westing Paper Products Corporation. She had been his legal adviser; she would inherit his stock and serve as a director of the company until the day she, too, would be elected chairman of the board.

Veiled in black, she hurried from the funeral services. It was Saturday and she had an important engagement. Angela brought her daughter, Alice, to the Wexler-Theodorakis mansion to spend Saturday afternoons with her aunt.

There she was, waiting for her in the library. Baba had tied red ribbons in the one long pigtail down her back.

"Hi there, Alice," T. R. Wexler said. "Ready for a game of chess?"